T0355027

The Rake's Redemption

SHERRILL BODINE

DIVERSIONBOOKS

For Jane and Sandra—who believe in us—thank you.

Diversion Books
A Division of Diversion Publishing Corp.
443 Park Avenue South, Suite 1008
New York, New York 10016
www.DiversionBooks.com

For more information, email info@diversionbooks.com

First Diversion Books edition December 2013.
Print ISBN: 978-1-62681-610-7
eBook ISBN: 978-1-62681-208-6

Prologue

CARSTAIR'S FOLLY, BERKSHIRE 1818

Dominic was bored. He turned away from contemplating the landscape by Constable over the fireplace and propped one shoulder against the mantel to survey the ruin of Carstair's dining room. Freddie might be his closest friend, his only true friend come to think of it, but still he should not have allowed himself to be convinced about this repairing lease with Carstair. Their idea of rusticating in the country hardly matched his own. When he tired of London, he wanted to be at Culter Towers. But even after ten years he couldn't go home without calling up bitter memories. So he had come into Berkshire to Carstair's Folly and found that Freddie had arranged a surprise—Yvette, his current favorite and two other ladybirds were waiting for them. It was not to be fishing and cards, but only the same routine as London.

Now he was the only member of the party still standing. Freddie, spread-eagled in a wing chair, had a wine glass resting upside down on his waistcoat, and their host Carstair, had slipped quietly under the table after they had broached the fourth bottle.

Where were the ladybirds? Focusing none too well, Dominic's eyes came to rest on two disheveled women, their unbound hair tangled over their faces, curled up at each end of the couch. But where was that minx, Yvette? Shaking his head, he blinked several times and found with surprise that his gait was slightly unsteady when he walked to the table, lifted the cloth, and peered beneath it. Yes, there she was asleep, one arm flung over Carstair's chest. He remembered now. She had joined Carstair there on the floor after complaining of

Dominic's neglect.

Shrugging, he let the cloth fall and reached for the half-empty bottle of port. She was right. He had not paid her the slightest heed. He poured port into a glass and tipped most of the contents down his throat. He shouldn't have come here. He should have gone home to Culter Towers to his grandparents. He missed them. But more than his yearly visit was still beyond him.

Tossing the remainder of the port down, he moved to the windows. It was dawn. Fog blanketed the lawn as it had that other dawn long ago, when he had strained to see through the mists. Suddenly he was there again—Culter Towers—with Jules.

They had stood with heads bent, separated by twin mounds of freshly turned earth, oblivious to the long queue of black-clad figures wending its way down a slight rise toward the massive towers of the stone manor house.

So suddenly and unexpectedly he was the Marquis of Aubrey. He'd been dressed in regimentals, with only two black arm bands to signify his mourning. Unsure of how to control the rage within, he'd stood clenching and unclenching his hands behind his back. "Father," he'd mouthed silently before lifting his face, eyes stinging with tears to glare across the two new graves unmarked by headstones.

Jules had leaned heavily on a walking stick. He was wearing superbly fitted black mourning clothes, but white bandages swathed his forehead and extended down the left side of his face, hiding any emotion that might be there.

"You're responsible for this." He had spat out the words, hate filling the space between them.

Jules stepped back a pace, staggering under the accusation, and turned to go.

"Brother!" His voice filled with menace had stopped Jules' attempted retreat. "Don't forget your promise. What has happened here ... is buried here."

A sneer had lifted one side of Jules's mouth throwing the rest of his face into a grotesque mask. "Oui, mon frère."

Rage burned in his heart. And hatred for the brother he had once loved. "I leave for the Peninsula tomorrow, and I want you off my lands as soon as you can travel. I never want to see you again!"

"Ah … but, you will see me again, I haven't forgotten this … Brother." One long white finger had lifted to fleetingly touch the bandage over the place his left eye should have been…

Dominic shivered, the rage and hatred still burning even after ten years. He'd been so young then—too young and too naive to have to face the secrets he'd had thrust at him the night his parents had died. So he'd fled to war to forget them. He wasn't naive anymore. Yet, he'd learned that one particular secret could never be forgotten.

The sun's light burst into the clearing before him. Another night gone. A fortnight of this—too much wine and no real pleasure—and even the familiar boredom of London would be welcome.

Glancing back over his shoulder at the room, sour with the scent of stale wine and cluttered with empty bottles and the remains of plates of food, he suddenly came to a decision.

Carstair's man, Sylvester, arrived an instant after Dominic rang and behind him, hovering in the hall, he could see both his own valet, Pringle, and Freddie's Timmings.

"You might as well all come in. You are needed," he drawled. "Sylvester, your master is under the dining table. Timmings, put Lord Liscombe to bed and when he awakens this afternoon, inform him we leave for London at first light."

Timmings gingerly removed the glass from Freddie's waistcoat and carefully examined it for stains before waking his master.

Sylvester summoned three footmen, two of whom crawled under the table to assist Lord Carstair. Having achieved their goal of getting him in an upright position, they handed him over to his long suffering butler. The third went to Timmings' aid and half carried Freddie from the room.

Pringle stood, his face utterly expressionless, not wishing to disturb his master, until finally he could contain his curiosity no longer. He coughed apologetically and glanced around the room. "Do I understand we are all leaving for town, my lord?"

Yawning, Dominic leaned back against the mantel, shutting his eyes. "A bit boring here, Pringle. Have my curricle ready in the morning. You and Timmings can go ahead with the baggage."

When Pringle coughed again, it grated a bit upon Dominic's nerves, but he did not open his eyes. "The ... ladies ... will they not be returning to London?"

He did open his lids then, staring at Pringle's impassive face. "Carstair arranged their arrival. He can arrange for their departure. It is of no concern to me."

Pushing himself away from the mantel, he stepped lazily over his former mistress, tucked a five-pound note into her ample bosom, and strolled from the room.

Chapter 1

WENTWORTH PARK, BERKSHIRE

The lady and gentleman seated in the high-ceilinged and airy library of Wentworth Park on an unusually warm afternoon in April were engaged in writing letters. Suddenly Juliana Grenville looked up and cleared her throat to speak in a low, soft voice, "George…"

He appeared not to have noticed her, so she spoke louder, "Brother dear…" Then louder, "George!"

George Vane, fifth Baron Wentworth, continued to write, neither looking up nor betraying by even the smallest sign that he had heard. Indeed, his head of red-gold curls drooped even more intently over the estate papers littering the desk.

Juliana waited a moment more, but when she spied the deep furrow creasing her brother's youthful brow, she rose to her feet, smoothed the folds of her second-best pink dimity morning dress, and crossed quickly to place her palms firmly onto the rim of the wide dark walnut desk. "George, Aunt Sophia and I are going to London. We plan to open Wentworth House for the Season."

Still his hand continued moving across the papers, although he did briefly glance up at her. "Wentworth House hasn't been open since father died two years ago. Old Smithers would turn up his toes if he had to get it ready." He shook his head, his gaze returning to his desk. "Go shopping in Basingstoke instead, Ju. Always been fond of it."

Juliana straightened her shoulders and drew up to her full height, which was, she lamented, regretfully short. "George, I have already written Smithers that we arrive in three days. I go to London in search of a husband."

She had caught his complete attention at last. His head jerked upward and his light green eyes, much like her own, widened in shock. "Good God, Juliana, what nonsense is this? Find a husband, indeed! Anytime these past five years you could have married." His eyes narrowed, causing fine lines to map his lean face and suddenly he looked much older than his twenty-one years. "Have you formed an attachment unknown to me?"

Juliana recognized the stubborn tilt of her brother's chin. It reminded her forcibly of their late father, when he had wished to be difficult. It was too soon for George to develop such habits, she thought, and too soon for his young face to show the marks of worry and responsibility. All the more reason why she must carry through with the plan Aunt Sophia had so fortuitously devised.

Juliana faced George across the desk and, although he was now the head of the family, he was younger by three years so had for most of his life accepted orders from her.

Deliberately he sprawled, apparently very much at ease, his fine lawn shirt open at the throat, his legs stretched out before him, and stared into her determined face. "There's no need to go to London. Soon as I spread the word every eligible man in the county will be on the doorstep," he drawled.

"You shall not put me to the blush, George. I am already acquainted with all the eligible men in the county. There are none here who suit my needs."

"Indeed!" Her brother squinted at her, another deep crease forming across his high forehead. "Then there is someone in particular!"

"Yes, I do have someone in mind." Juliana paused, letting her words sink in slowly as George's face turned a rich ruby red. Oh, yes, it was more than time to implement the plan! "An older man, I think. A lonely widower with children who need a mother. Such a man would suit my purpose quite well I believe."

"Damn it, Ju!" he shouted, leaping to his feet. "That sounds like someone to suit Aunt Sophia!"

"Aunt Sophia has said she shall not remarry."

"I know," her brother answered without hesitation, "but you've said the same thing."

"I find that my feelings have undergone a change in the last six years. Someday you will wed and no longer need me. I would find someone who does."

"What about Sir Lionel? Been dangling after you forever. He needs you to run the Grange. Never seen a man who wanted more help," George answered swiftly.

Juliana took a deceptively casual turn about the elegant room. She was prepared to argue her point, having considered and rejected every possible man in the county in previous discussions with Aunt Sophia. She stopped to gaze at the forbidding portrait of her father over the mantel. He'd not have allowed that connection, but Sir Lionel was George's friend, so she must be careful.

"Yes, George. Lionel does need an estate manager. However, I do not feel I could be a good wife to a man who lisps."

"By Gad. You're right, Ju! Forgotten that." He squinted across the room at the Reynolds portrait of their mother on horseback. "How about Jonathan Long? No lisp there and a very pretty seat. In fact, I've heard you say Courtney Manor is the prettiest place you've seen bar Wentworth."

"A delightful boy, George, but two years my junior. Since his return from London, I find him very difficult to converse with. He can't seem to turn his head for the height of his shirt points."

"But Jonathan is in the height of fashion, he says. You're always wanting me to go to London and be part of the *ton.*"

"I fear that shall be my fate instead, for I've considered all my acquaintances and no one seems to answer. Aunt Sophia assures me that a Season is the perfect solution. After all, her engagement to Uncle Corny was announced before her first Season ended. I'm quite determined that I will no longer be a burden to you. I must leave Wentworth Park and get on with my life, and Aunt Sophia says London is just the place to do so."

Moving quickly, George placed his slender hands on her shoulders, his face once again young and engaging in his eagerness. "Don't be a goose, Ju. You'll always be wanted here.

Wentworth Park is as much your home as mine. No need to sacrifice yourself on the marriage mart. Parson's Mousetrap ain't for me. Like things just as they are. Plan to go on like this forever!"

Juliana laughed, reaching up to place a kiss on her brother's chin before moving away to the open French doors where a slight breeze ruffled the curtains. The afternoon air was light and soft with fluffy clouds that allowed the sun to warm the earth in pale golden streams. The lawns of Wentworth Park stretched before her as smooth as green velvet. The scent of flowering peach trees filled the air, and in the distance she could see Zeke, the gardener, lovingly bending over tender spring blooms.

How could she bear to leave this? All of her memories were tied to this one place: warm but vague memories of a sweet-faced mother, happy memories of a carefree childhood, tender memories of the sweet torment of Will's courtship. Those weeks of living for a glance of him, elation when he appeared and despair when he took his leave.

How young they had been! Perhaps too young to have married. But that brief month of their marriage before he left for the Peninsula was the dearest memory of all. She clung to it as she did this place.

Yet now, finally, it was time to let go. She and Aunt Sophia had talked long about George's future. He had been left the responsibility for the Park too soon and had taken his duty so seriously he had immersed himself in the running of the estate. He had learned quickly, so that now all the hours he spent worrying and fussing were only habit. Aunt Sophia was firmly convinced that the only way to draw George away from his devotion to the Park so that he could take his place in the *ton* was to lure him to London on the pretext of finding Juliana a husband. It was not in Juliana's nature to lie, but she was prepared to do so for her brother's sake.

Taking a short, strengthening breath of the fresh spring air, she turned to face George, forcing her mouth to curve in a smile. "It is hardly a sacrifice to place myself on the marriage mart and come away with a prize. I hope I have not become such an antidote that I cannot find a husband."

Her words brought a derisive snort from her brother before he grabbed her hand and pulled her laughingly across the room to a large gilt mirror hung over a highly polished cherry wood chest. He stood behind her, his fingers curling over her shoulders.

They were much alike, the same thick, vibrant auburn curls, slanting spring green eyes set over high cheekbones, but George was tall and lean, whereas she was small and softly rounded.

Their eyes met in the glass.

"When you were seventeen and married Will, all my friends were calf-eyed over you." Her brother's voice was low and gentle. "They still are. Every eligible man in the county has told me you're beautiful." Suddenly he grinned. "Don't get missish, Ju. You're no antidote and you know it."

She caught his grin, twining her fingers through his where they rested on her shoulders, confident now that her scheme would work just as she and Aunt Sophia had planned. "Please understand, George dear. I find that I want what other women want. A husband … and … and a family. Lady Grenville has made it abundantly clear that even though I am a widow, propriety demands I have a female chaperon, which is why Aunt Sophia has remained here."

George threw back his head in a hearty laugh. "Aunt Sophia, a chaperon! Why, she won't keep tabs on you at all."

"Yes, George, I know," Juliana interjected quickly. "That's why it's most important for you to come to London and lend me countenance. Your assessment of character would be a great help in weeding out potential suitors."

He looked puzzled for an instant, but then gave her again his charmingly rueful smile. "Perhaps I will. I must confess you've taken me by surprise, Ju. I thought you'd never get over your feelings for Will."

"Of course, I haven't gotten over them!" The words were out before she could stop them. Schooling her face to reflect nothing of her feelings, she continued with a wistful smile, "Will is always first in my heart. But I am still going to London to find a husband."

• , • •

"Aunt Sophia, it went just as you said it would." Juliana burst through her aunt's bedroom door to stop in bewilderment at the piles of clothing strewn about. "Why, whatever are you doing? I thought you'd already packed."

"No need to keep these old things." Sophia waved her hand vaguely in the air. "I thought I'd leave them for the reverend to distribute. We'll be getting all new."

"All new?" Juliana asked quizzingly.

Her aunt crossed the room sprightly to envelop her in strong arms. "It will be such fun. I can't wait to see you in the latest fashions. You'll find everything we have is sadly outdated. I want you to cut quite a figure in the *ton*, as I did," she added dreamily.

Sophia was a pleasant-faced woman of undistinguished appearance until she smiled, and then, as a suitor had once said, "It was like a burst of sunshine," making her eyes sparkle a silvery gray and causing a small dimple to appear beside her mouth. That delightful smile played across her face now as she clasped Juliana's hands and danced around the room.

"I suddenly feel quite young again, myself," she laughed.

A gentle tap sounded and Sophia stopped abruptly.

"Come in, Maitland."

"No, it's me, Charlotte," came the gentle reply from a tall, willowy girl, whose red-rimmed eyes dominated her pale face. Escaping blond wisps of hair tangled in disarray, and her royal blue riding hat hung from its ribbons around her shoulders.

"My dear, what's amiss?" Sophia darted forward to draw her gently into the room.

"It's Mama. She says I must spend all my time in London being nice to some old man." She sniffed.

"What is Lady Grenville about now?" Sophia demanded.

Juliana cast a speaking look at her aunt before patting Charlotte's arm. "Now, now, this isn't like you at all. You usually handle your mama quite well," Juliana soothed.

"Usually, but this time she's determined to marry me off to some distant, second cousin who'll be a duke one day."

"It won't be so dreadful being in London for the Season," Juliana smiled intriguingly. "Aunt and I will be there to rescue you. Our plan worked."

"George," Charlotte ventured quietly, "George will be in London for my Season?"

Juliana triumphed. "Eventually. He'll be there as soon as that new strain of wheat takes. He refuses to leave for another fortnight." She turned to watch her aunt again ruthlessly sorting through the wardrobe. "Aunt Sophia insists that we leave as planned, since we have so much to do before the Season starts."

Charlotte brightened immediately. "I believe I saw George riding toward the south field on my way here. Our estate agent thinks the new strain is just slow to germinate. Perhaps I should ride out and tell him myself."

Juliana's lifted brows registered her surprise as Charlotte suddenly rushed from the room. Turning to Sophia, she remarked, "Why haven't I realized Charlotte was developing a tendre for George?"

"You have been concerned with other matters," her aunt stated simply.

"You're right, dearest. There has been so much tragedy at Wentworth Park. George grew up before I knew what was happening … Will's death … followed so quickly by his father's … then my papa's death." Juliana shook her head slowly, a hint of moisture on her long lashes, before she caught herself and with a few rapid blinks, smiled. "Listen to me, carrying on like a ninnyhammer."

"So right, love," Sophia agreed matter-of-factly, determined to change the subject immediately. She felt Juliana had shed enough tears to last a lifetime. It was the chief reason she'd devised the now-famous plan. "However, I should point out you neglected to mention Lady Grenville in your list of tragedies."

"Aunt! How can you!" Juliana's perfectly arched brows rose. "After Will died on the Peninsula, Sir Alfred and Lady Grenville had every right to his estate. After all, Sir Alfred is the last male Grenville."

"My dear, I said nothing against Sir Alfred. How could I? A

more unoffensive man I have never met. One barely knows he is even there. It is his revolting wife I cannot tolerate."

"I am quite sure Lady Grenville has some good qualities." Juliana stopped, her cherry lips blossoming into a sudden smile. "She must have at least one good quality, mustn't she?"

Sophia laughed. "She is Charlotte's mother, so she must be doing something right—a very unique child."

"Dear Charlotte! I look forward to seeing her in London. We can only hope Lady Grenville does not make her first Season too tedious."

Early the next day, content that her own secret plan to get Juliana away from the sad memories and into the *ton* had succeeded, Sophia Thatcher leaned back against the crimson squabs of their luxurious traveling coach and surveyed her niece. Juliana's mouth curved with a small, secret smile as she peered out onto the pleasant Berkshire countryside they traveled through.

The spring rain had ceased two days earlier. Now brooks gurgled merrily over their banks and purple violets and daisies eagerly pushed through the young meadow grass. Birds sang to one another from the low hanging branches of elm trees bordering the road. With pleasure Juliana breathed in spring and laughed softly.

"You have every reason to be smug. My congratulations," Sophia complimented. "Wellington himself could not have maneuvered so well, my dear. I can't believe George is at last going to forsake his cattle and crops for the pleasures of London."

"Is it not marvelous, Aunt?" Juliana's eyes flashed with happiness. "He feels honor bound to join us in London, since you are such a lamentable chaperon."

"The dear boy has turned into a deplorable prig for one so young. Just like your father. I will never forget the first time I let you ride without a groom. I thought your father would have an apoplexy." Sophia chuckled. "Such foolishness!"

The heavy traveling coach lurched when its right rear wheel

caught in a deep rut formed during the recent rains. It tilted crazily and instinctively both ladies grabbed for a strap. Sophia gasped in surprise when a crimson pillow flew past her cheek as the coach toppled precariously to the right. She slid against the door frame and the coach succumbed to gravity.

Juliana reached for her but missed, losing her own balance, and struck her head on the door frame landing heavily on Sophia's outstretched leg as they both tumbled to the floor.

Juliana's heart was banging loudly against her chest. The jolt she had received when her head struck the wooden door came sweeping over her in a paralyzing aftershock so that she lay motionless until a slight movement and a loud moan brought her to her senses.

Aunt Sophia! She must be hurting Aunt Sophia!

Benjamin, the coachman, appeared in the open doorway. "Oi, miss, be you all right!" His face creasing into dozens of worried lines, he reached in, his two thick, burly arms lifting her out and to the ground.

Juliana closed her eyes for only a moment, the side of her head throbbing painfully, before she clutched at the coach door, calling "Aunt Sophia!"

Her aunt's face appeared suddenly from beneath a crimson pillow. "Here I am, dear," she replied calmly, reaching out both hands. "Benjamin, I believe I need your help."

Juliana felt ridiculously weak. But using what little strength she possessed, she helped Benjamin ease her aunt from the precariously tilting coach, which groaned menacingly, shifting even deeper into the mud when they pulled Sophia to safety.

To her great relief Sophia appeared unhurt, except for a long rip in the skirt of her dove gray traveling gown and a ruined blue feather dropping over the bent rim of her once fashionable hat.

"I am quite all right. There is no need for this fuss," Sophia said before taking a deep, shaky breath. "However, I do believe I must sit down, for this was a bit more excitement than I bargained for."

"It warn't really my fault, Miss Juliana," Benjamin blubbered.

"The pole must've snapped with all that jouncing."

"It's all right, Benjamin," Juliana soothed, anxious only to see her aunt comfortable. "Let us settle Aunt Sophia under that tree."

With Benjamin carefully taking most of Sophia's weight against his broad shoulder, Juliana helped her slowly to the shade of an elm tree several yards from where young Ben, the postboy, held the still rearing and stomping horses.

Lumbering back to the coach, Benjamin stroked an experienced palm over the sweating side of one of the chestnuts. Juliana knew he loved his horses and would have no trouble calming them. She was more concerned about caring for her aunt so far from help. Searching in vain through her reticule for a restorative, she frowned, angry with herself, and looked up at Sophia, but that good woman was calmly fanning herself with the ruins of her traveling hat.

"Juliana, love, don't look so distressed."

Slumping down beside her, Juliana untied the wide blue satin ribbons on her own crushed bonnet. "What a beginning for our journey!"

Juliana leaned her head to one side in the hope *of* easing the painful throbbing at her temple, which was worsening, so that she spied Benjamin unharnessing the horses through a filmy haze. Nevertheless, she pushed herself to her feet, leaving her aunt resting on the cool grass. She made her way carefully, for the earth seemed to be slightly unsettled under her boots, to where he was tying one of the chestnuts to a sturdy looking sapling.

"What can be done, Benjamin?" she asked softly.

Carefully, he peered both ways down the muddy road. "Best for me to go for help, Miss Juliana. Axle done for." He looked at her from under his thick, sandy eyebrows. "Be you all right? Young Ben will stand guard ... Lad!" he bellowed and Ben ran forward, his face as red as the thatch of hair sticking out in a profusion of cowlicks all over his small head. "Be you on watch while I go for help." He placed a heavy hand on his son's slim shoulder. "Can you do it, lad?"

"I ain't afrait!" Young Ben lifted his chin, gazing solemnly at his father. "You go on, Pa. I'll take care of Miss Juliana."

Although the throbbing at her temple caused her to feel light-headed and nausea sat heavily in her stomach, Juliana forced a smile, placing a caressing hand on ten-year-old Ben's unruly curls. "Yes, you must go, Benjamin. We shall be fine here until you return."

Benjamin nodded, swinging himself upon the untethered chestnut, and cast a last stern look at his son before turning and galloping down the road.

Ben looked up at her, his toothy grin causing her to feel a great rush of affection. "This be a great adventure, ain't it, Miss Juliana?"

She hugged his thin, wiry body to her side, then glanced to where Sophia sat fanning herself, and finally down into Ben's excited face. The peacefulness of Wentworth Park seemed very far away and, at this moment, very, very dear indeed.

The sun was just beginning to invade the small square of shade where they rested when a glistening curricle drawn by a pair of matched grays swept past them. Juliana lifted her hand, shading her eyes, to watch the driver bring the team to a neat halt, expertly turn them, and drive back to where they sat. Whoever he was, Juliana couldn't help but admire his superb driving skill.

Ben, however, was not lost in admiration. He leapt to his feet, taking a firm grip on the large stick with which he had been idly digging pictures in the mud.

She rose to put her hands on his rigidly held shoulders. "You needn't worry, Ben. These gentlemen appear quite harmless."

The gentlemen looked just as occupants of such a racy curricle ought. The shorter of the two walked toward them, his black Hessians gleaming, his bottlegreen jacket fitting his wide shoulders to perfection.

Pausing beside his horses, the driver's face was lost in the glare of the sun. "Here, lad, attend to the team!" he demanded.

His voice held such a note of authority that Ben did not hesitate for a moment. He ran to do as he was bidden, the stick forgotten in the dirt.

Juliana knew someone had to hold the horses, but the

driver's autocratic manner struck her as a bit arrogant. He has no right to order Ben! He may be rescuing us, but he needn't be so overbearing. She took a sudden dislike to the faceless stranger and thrust up her chin. Making a point of ignoring the driver, she turned back to her aunt.

The shorter gentleman with the wide, cheerful face and the light, fluffy brown curls had knelt beside Aunt Sophia.

"May I be of service?" he asked, his hazel eyes round with concern. "I'm Lord Freddie Liscombe, and this is the Marquis of Aubrey," he said, glancing over his shoulder at the driver, who finally relinquished the reins to Ben.

Although she pretended to pay the Marquis of Aubrey no heed, she did steal a peek from beneath her lashes to watch him walk toward them, but all she could see were his Hessians, only slightly smudged from the muddy road.

Finally she decided to acknowledge him. Tilting her head, she slowly looked up and her eyes widened. She had never been a great worshiper of male beauty, not even as a very young girl, but the marquis possessed a face so arresting that he could be called beautiful in a uniquely male way. She felt a confusing blend of fear and delight that so startled her, she literally ceased breathing for an instant. He was above medium height, his dark chocolate velvet jacket fit smoothly over broad shoulders, revealing hard, flowing muscles that rippled across his back when he bent over her aunt. His burnished head turned a dozen shades of gold in the sunlight, his long, firm mouth turned up at the corners, a dimple appeared in his chin, and his heavy cornflower blue eyes, spaciously set, looked straight into hers.

Good God, she was staring at him! The throbbing at her temples increased so that she had to close her eyes for a moment against the bright sun as the terrible dizziness assailed her again. A pair of light, strong hands steadied her, but released her when her lids flew open and she stepped away.

"Are you all right?" asked the Marquis of Aubrey, his wonderful face radiating sympathy.

Juliana only nodded, confused by this show of concern after his autocratic commands only a moment before, attempting to recover her wits and find her tongue, which seemed to be tied. She stood like a ninny staring at the marquis.

"I'm Mrs. Sophia Thatcher and this is my niece, Juliana. As you can see, we've suffered a mishap."

Juliana went limp with relief when Sophia's voice broke the silence. Both gentlemen performed neat bows and, the spell broken, Juliana took a shuddering breath as the Marquis of Aubrey turned to their ruined carriage.

Lord Liscombe shook his head. "By jove, it's really done for!" he said with a grimace before joining in a swift inspection of the broken axle wheel and their once fashionable coach now resting deeply in the mire.

Juliana's head started to ache again, deep throbs pounding up the back of her neck. Feeling too weak to stand and face the marquis as she longed to—on equal territory—she sunk slowly to the ground.

Her usually pleasant countenance creased in a small frown, Sophia reached out to touch Juliana's hands. "Are you all right, love? You look pale."

"I'm quite well," she murmured softly, disciplining herself not to show in any way that the pain throbbing in her head was nearly unbearable. "I only wish Benjamin would hurry."

Her words were caught by the marquis. "Your coachman has gone to the Blue Boar for help?"

"If that is the nearest inn, yes, my lord, he has," she answered with a firmness she just mustered, priding herself on how smoothly she rose to her feet.

She lifted her chin, unaware that her three companions could plainly see the discomfort marring her flushed face. The marquis's eyes remained fixed on her and her spine tingled when his gaze flickered over her, so she held her shoulders unnaturally straight, concentrating on the pain throbbing at her temples, willing it to go away. Instead the darkening world pitched and spun, and for the first time in her life she fell into a dead faint.

• • •

Juliana felt warm and very secure. She attempted to open her eyes, but failed for her lids were too heavy. Rather desperately she fought the languishing stupor of her body, to concentrate on bringing herself into a more stable orbit. Her lashes lifted slowly and her world was filled with deep, rich chocolate velvet much like the jacket the marquis had been wearing. Tilting her head just the tiniest bit, her world expanded to include cornflower blue.

"How beautiful your eyes are," she heard herself whisper. His thick, silky lashes lazily flickered and his eyes seemed to expand and lighten, but she closed her lids against their brilliance, for the dark mist was again swirling at the edges of her consciousness. Tucking her cheek back onto that one certain spot felt so right, she sighed deeply and once more let the mist of darkness envelop her.

Chapter 2

Surprise stilled Dominic's hand as he reached for the half-empty tankard of ale. Surprise at the depth of feeling he'd experienced carrying Juliana when he had held countless beautiful women in his arms and felt nothing. When she had opened her eyes, whispered to him, and then snuggled again trustingly into his arms, he had been shocked by the rush of tenderness he'd felt. Women usually were not so trusting around the Marquis of Aubrey. Arch, yes. Coy, definitely. Calculating. He had learned to deal with women who always seemed to want something from him. But this was different. This young woman had not expected anything, instead she had given her trust to a stranger.

Dominic wondered at his reluctance to move away after laying her on the feather quilt in the bright chamber upstairs. Finally he had removed his arms and backed slowly until he reached the door, wanting her to open those luminous green eyes again—to be sure that the trusting innocence would still be there. But Mrs. Forbes, the innkeeper's grandmother, had firmly shut the door on him. He'd walked down to the taproom, careful to stay within call should he be needed.

"Dom!" Freddie hailed from the hallway.

"In here, Freddie," Dominic answered, leaning back to stretch at ease in one of the comfortable armchairs set around the fireplace in the taproom of the Blue Boar.

Freddie's face was flushed with impatience. "Dom, the horses are standing. If we're to be in London by tonight, we should leave."

"I think we'll stay here for the night." He slowed his voice to its habitual drawl. "The ale is quite good."

"And Juliana's a dashed pretty girl," Freddie snapped back.

Dominic lifted one eyebrow sardonically. The disdain written across his face was not wasted on his best friend.

Sighing, Freddie shrugged. "You're right, of course. It'd be damn ungallant of us to leave before the poor girl's even awake."

Consciousness returned with the scent of roses. Juliana opened her eyes to the late afternoon sun slanting through small window panes in a room she had never seen before. Turning her head wearily, she found with relief that the terrible pain was gone and saw her aunt sitting, peacefully knitting, in front of a stone fireplace.

Memory returned to her and with it a curious dread that she had taken the first step down an unfamiliar and frightening path. Where was she? And how did she come to be in this pleasant low-ceilinged bedchamber?

Anxiety made her sit up suddenly, glancing around for her blue merino traveling gown. "Where are we? And how did I get here?"

Sophia looked at her as if it was the most normal thing in the world for her to awaken in a strange bed with nothing but her chemise covering her.

"You are awake at last, love."

"What happened! And where are my clothes?" she asked in alarm.

"One question at a time," laughed Sophia. "We are at the Blue Boar Inn. And the Marquis of Aubrey carried you here."

"The marquis carried me!" Juliana sunk back onto the surprisingly soft pillows, a groan rising in her throat.

A smile came into Sophia's eyes. "Well, yes. He could hardly do less after you so neatly fainted right into his arms."

"I felt sure it was only a dream," she mused in a hopeful voice, "that at one point I appeared to enjoy being carried."

Sophia gave her head a small shake.

"I thought as much." Juliana closed her eyes, a wave of acute, hot embarrassment making her again feel ill.

She felt Sophia sit on the side of the bed. "No need for

worry, love," her aunt said, gently stroking back Juliana's tousled auburn curls and touching with great care the sore spot on her temple. "When we discovered the lump on your forehead, we realized you were not yourself."

"I have a lump on my forehead!" Juliana's lids flew open. "Tell me the truth, Aunt Sophia. Do I also have a black eye?"

"I do detect a bruise over your eyebrow, my dear. But nothing to signify."

She had never been overly vain, but the vision of confronting the splendor of the Marquis of Aubrey and his friend Lord Liscombe with a great lump upon her head, and an unsightly bruise above her eye lowered her spirits considerably. The happy thought came to her that, perhaps, they had already departed. When asked, Sophia brightened with a smile.

"Of course not, love. They were both most concerned about you." Patting Juliana's hand she rose from the bed. "When I'm downstairs preparing your gruel, I will inform them that you are awake. And I'll tell Mrs. Forbes that her headache potion was successful."

Her aunt moved briskly toward the door. "Aunt Sophia, who is Mrs. Forbes?"

Sophia drew back into the room and clapped her hands in delight. "She is a marvel, my dear! I was quite frantic when you fainted, but she took one look at you and declared her potion would cure you. And so it has. Before we leave, remind me to get the recipe."

Juliana lay back, dazed by her aunt's bright spirits, and fell promptly asleep.

A short time later the door opened waking her instantly. Sophia came in bearing a tray with a bowl, a spoon, a pristine white napkin, and a single, perfect red rose. She set the tray across Juliana's lap and handed her the napkin. Juliana noticed an unusual sparkle in her aunt's normally serene gray eyes.

She hesitated, but couldn't keep herself from asking, "Wherever did you find such a lovely rose?"

"I did not," replied her aunt. "Freddie asked for permission to cut it from Mrs. Forbes's rose garden, which is below our window. I thought it quite sweet of him."

The marquis's marvelous face flashed through her mind, and Juliana was aware of a slight feeling of disappointment, but she instantly put such thoughts from her. "Yes, very considerate," she said brightly. "But, Aunt, when did you begin calling Lord Liscombe, Freddie?"

"Oh, we are quite comfortable with one another now, my dear. You were asleep for several hours, you know. I allow them to call me Sophia. And they have asked me to call them Freddie and Dominic ... you know, Juliana," her aunt stood, chewing on her lower lip, a habit she had whenever her memory failed her. "Dominic reminds me of someone. Something in the way he speaks or moves. And his name ... I'm sure it has a familiar ring to it." A frown marred her pleasant countenance. "I have this dreadful feeling that it is extremely important for me to remember where I have heard of him."

The next morning Sophia was still trying to recall why Dominic seemed so familiar. Juliana was tempted to tell her that the marquis was not the kind of man who could be easily forgotten, but decided not to feed her aunt's interest. To tell the truth, she could not share Sophia's excitement that their two rescuers were still in attendance. She was not a fanciful young woman; indeed, her father had often told her she was alarmingly pragmatic, but she found the marquis ... unsettling. Which was why she felt shy at the breakfast hour, even though she had pinched her cheeks so that they had a tinge of color and had skillfully pulled an auburn curl forward to hide both her lump and bruise. She found the marquis and Lord Liscombe in the small private parlor with her aunt, who had preceded her by a few minutes, when Juliana felt the need to spend a bit more time on her toilette.

"We have been waiting for you, love." Both gentlemen rose to their feet as Sophia gestured toward the chair nearest her.

Lord Liscombe eyed her with undisguised appreciation, which did bring back a little of her usual confidence. "Good morning, Juliana."

24

The marquis sketched a bow and Juliana, her face feeling stiff from her forced smile, sat down next to her aunt.

"We have just been sampling Mrs. Forbes's marvelous tea. The woman is a genius in the kitchen," Sophia remarked serenely.

"I'd say so," promptly replied Lord Liscombe. "Dominic offered her a place in charge of his kitchen in town, but she turned him down. Flat!" Crowing with laughter, Freddie's round hazel eyes were as bright as new buttons. "Even the legendary Aubrey charm couldn't change her mind."

"Indeed!" Relaxing a bit more, Juliana glanced at the marquis and found it difficult to believe any woman could refuse him when he set out to be charming.

Dominic Crawford, Marquis of Aubrey, heir to one of England's oldest and wealthiest dukedoms, felt his boredom lift. There was a decided sparkle of amusement in Juliana's lovely eyes, and his interest, tickled at the first sight of her and aroused when she cuddled in his arms like a purring kitten, had been most definitely caught. He placed his cup firmly on its saucer. "Yes. She informed me that she could not allow herself to be dictated to by a demanding schoolboy."

"Schoolboy!" Juliana's perfect brows rose in apparent delight to meet her glossy curls. He could still remember the fragrance of her hair, fresh, clean, and slightly perfumed when it had fallen over his chest.

His lips twitched and his eyes watched the play of emotions across her face. "Yes. Mrs. Forbes is our innkeeper's grandmother. Not his wife. She views all of us in much the same way she does Robbie." Seeing Juliana's inquiring look, he added, "Mr. Forbes. His grandmother refers to him either as Robbie or lad."

The marquis remarked that in many ways Mrs. Forbes was a great deal like his own grandmama. Juliana was never to discover where this interesting thought might have led, for the parlor door opened and a robust young serving girl carrying an enormous tray entered. Kidneys grilled to perfection, succulent chops, eggs plucked fresh from the henhouse that very morning, flaky, marvelous-smelling rolls, jams and jellies, and more of Mrs. Forbes's strong, rich tea was laid out before them.

Some time later, Sophia sighed, leaning back in her chair. "That was truly wonderful. I shall miss Mrs. Forbes's tea. I do hope she will share that secret with me."

Juliana laid down her napkin, feeling much stronger after eating, ready to again take charge. "Recipes will wait, Aunt Sophia. First we must inquire from Benjamin about our coach."

"I've already spoken to him," Dominic stated, causing Juliana's eyes to widen in surprise. Her first assumption had been correct. The man was overbearing! If he sensed her surprise at his presumption, it did not seem to bother him in the slightest, for he continued in the same casual voice. "A new pole is needed. The wheelwright told Benjamin it will take at least two days to repair. But I would be happy to send to London for one of my own coaches. It could be here by tomorrow morning."

A faint clucking from Sophia indicated her dismay, but Juliana lifted her chin, returning the marquis's level look. "Thank you, my lord. But we would not think of inconveniencing you. Aunt Sophia and I shall be quite comfortable here until our coach is repaired."

"Whatever will you do to amuse yourselves for two days?" Freddie asked in frank bewilderment.

"We shall walk in the lovely gardens I saw below my bedroom window, copy Mrs. Forbes's excellent recipes, perhaps, even picnic in the woods. It shall be quite pleasant!" Juliana declared, glaring at the marquis, defying him to disagree.

A smile played at the corners of Dominic's lips. Juliana was not in the usual fashion of women of his acquaintance. That in itself was an enticement. "Indeed, Juliana, that sounds most intriguing. So much so, that I believe Freddie and I will break our journey here for a day or two."

At his words Juliana's face became a delight, the long-lashed slanting eyes widened and her luscious, full lower lip fell open slightly.

Freddie directed an astonished look at him, which he blandly returned. "But Timmings only packed three fresh neck cloths! Told you it wasn't a good idea to send Pringle and Timmings ahead to London from Carstair's hunting box." He gestured toward Dominic. "Of course, you as creator of the Aubrey Nonpareil haven't a problem. But I need Timmings's touch to accomplish a respectable fold."

Sophia smiled complacently. "Nonsense, Freddie. Your cravat is all we could ask for. Besides, our lady's maid has gone ahead of us, too. So we can be quite comfortable and informal here."

"Sophia is right, Freddie. And if need be, I'll teach you my trick for the Waterfall," Dominic offered lazily.

Freddie's response was ludicrously serious. "Is that so, Dom? Why now after all the times I've asked before?"

"Because it pleases me now. As it pleases me to stay here with this charming company. After all, there is nothing pressing to attend to in London." It was true. The endless soirees, gaming halls, and bagnios in which he sought surcease were not of the least importance.

Juliana was a dazzler, and she intrigued him. She appeared to know nothing about him, so for these few days he would allow himself the pleasure of her company. No doubt, by then he would have his answer. She was either an exceptional actress who was playing her cards just right to interest him, or she would reveal herself to be as boring as all the other women of his acquaintance. Then he would be eager for London. But not just yet.

His eyes encountered Sophia's for a fleeting instant, just long enough for him to catch the glimmer of her amused smile. She rose from the table, picking out the folds of her gown. "That will be quite pleasant, Dominic. Now, I believe I shall begin in the kitchen with Mrs. Forbes. She spoke of gathering herbs that I might take to London with me." She turned to her niece. "There is a stone bench in the center of the garden. You should rest there in the sun this morning, love, but be sure to take your sunshade."

Doing his best to engage Juliana's attention, Freddie hovered beside her. "I would be most happy…"

"To assist Sophia in gathering herbs," finished Dominic, a man famed for his sword play.

Freddie shot him a withering look, which had no affect whatsoever. Dominic sat draped back in his chair, his long legs stretched in front of him.

With a nearly inaudible sigh, Freddie offered Sophia his arm and swept her out of the room, casting a last exasperated look at Dominic before shutting the parlor door with a bit more force than absolutely necessary.

Finding himself alone with Juliana, a situation no chaperon in London would have allowed for an instant, especially given his reputation, Dominic was surprised to see her square her shoulders and look straight into his eyes. She looked proud, resentful, and begrudgingly grateful. She looked like a ruffled kitten.

"I would like to take this opportunity to thank you, my lord, for your assistance yesterday," she said properly.

"It was my pleasure." He deliberately kept his face and voice utterly innocent, but still a rush of color stained her lovely cheeks. He thought perhaps she recalled how she had snuggled against him, apparently enjoying being carried so intimately by a stranger.

Nodding, she stood and moved quickly away from the table, but in one fluid motion he was in front of her. He could not allow her to leave him so quickly. Smiling, he took her hand leading her through the door, down the hall, and out into the sunlight before she quite realized what was happening.

Mrs. Forbes's garden was one of the loveliest spots Juliana had ever seen. Pink, white, and yellow roses climbed the low rosy brick wall of the courtyard. A burst of blue and white asters bordered the kitchen garden, so the scent of flowering trees, roses, and herbs mingled warmly.

Goodness, Juliana, what are you doing! she scolded herself and hastily withdrew her fingers from his firm grasp where she had allowed them to rest. She seated herself on the cool stone bench, clasped her hands in her lap, and raised her eyes calmly to his face. "Thank you, my lord marquis."

He gave her another slow—Juliana blushed to even think it—beckoning smile. "Will you object to my sitting with you for a moment?" he asked. She moved slightly to make room when he sat crowding the bench. He half turned toward her. "I trust you are feeling no more ill effects from your accident."

"No, indeed! Last night Mrs. Forbes sent me a sleeping draught so that when I awoke this morning I felt as good as new." She looked solemnly back into his arresting face and tried not to let it affect her pulse. "And, of course, Aunt Sophia's first bowl of gruel always has amazing restorative properties ... for one lives in mortal fear of the second."

Cornflower blue eyes lit with amusement. He reached toward her. Unable to help herself, Juliana stiffened, but he appeared not to notice as he plucked a rose from the bush directly behind her right shoulder.

The marquis smiled with luxurious charm, placing the pink rose, drops of dew still clinging to its petals, or her lap. "I prefer to deliver my flowers in person." His deep, rich voice made her feel decidedly warm.

"It is very lovely. Thank you," she murmured, raising the bloom to her lips. She had no idea why she should find it so difficult to behave normally around this man. After all, she was no green miss. She had been married!

Suddenly, from behind a clump of berry bushes, a tiny birdlike woman carrying an enormous garden basket appeared. The marquis rose to his feet giving the woman a smile that was, no doubt, famous throughout England. Although it had not been directed at Juliana, she felt its tug. Where was the arrogant, overbearing marquis? At the moment he looked very much like a sweet, slightly mischievous boy whom she wanted to hug. The woman with the garden basket obviously did not share her feelings.

She gave a crack of laughter. "Don't try your tricks with me, young lord. Won't work." Her mouth curved into a grin, causing her brown face to crease into a network of tiny lines. "Although you are bonny. More so than most."

Bowing deeply, the marquis took her thin, heavily veined fingers to his lips. "You are a joy, Mrs. Forbes. May I present Juliana, Sophia's niece."

Juliana had guessed that this woman could be none other than the redoubtable Mrs. Forbes. The vivid, dark brown eyes that surveyed her face were full of a lively intelligence. "Glad to meet you, young lady. I see my herb drink helped you."

"Very much! Thank you. I am most sorry for any inconvenience we have caused you."

"Nonsense," replied Mrs. Forbes in a practical spirit. "Good to have you young people here. Sophia's in the kitchen brewing up a sleeping draught now. Lord Liscombe is with her. That's why I came out here looking for these." She held out a palm full of garlic bulbs. "That young lord shows too many late nights and too many bottles of brandy. I have just the potion for him."

Juliana carefully controlled her face when Mrs. Forbes's eyes flickered across it and then to Dominic, whose unholy grin was nearly her undoing.

"Come along, both of you. Elixir must be brewed before you leave for London." Mrs. Forbes shook her head with such vigor, her large bun of grizzled white hair jiggled precariously. "Terrible place the city. Terrible!"

Was there ever a merrier look than the one the marquis flashed at her before bowing with a deep flourish and following Mrs. Forbes back into the kitchen.

The inn's kitchen was large. Fires blazed in enormous fireplaces at each end of the room, but the air was surprisingly fresh and cool, for a breeze worried the crisp curtains at huge windows on opposite walls. Rows of wooden shelves laden with jars of all sizes lined the stone walls and a long, polished oak table dominated the room. Aunt Sophia stood over a small black kettle slowly adding herbs to a boiling mixture while Freddie, coatless and with his shirt sleeves rolled up to his elbows, stirred with a long-handled wooden spoon.

So intent were they on their duties that they didn't notice Mrs. Forbes's entrance until she went to the pot to carefully examine the contents. She sniffed the steam. "Ah, yes. More mandrake root. Juliana, fetch that small jar of brown powder on the low shelf next to the window. Here, my lord marquis, chop these leaves."

Juliana watched Dominic shrug out of his coat, paying earnest attention to Mrs. Forbes's instruction of the precise method to chop herbs. Smiling, Juliana crossed toward the shelves. At the window she noticed white and red cloth balls hanging. She expected to find the scent of cloves and cinnamon, but moving closer discovered the balls scentless.

Frowning, she carried the small jar back to the table. "That is odd, Mrs. Forbes, your pomanders have no scent."

"Not pomanders, young lady. It is my herb potion to keep out insects."

Brushing a droopy brown curl from her forehead, Aunt Sophia turned from her pot. "Ingenious! I noticed that the kitchen was free of such troublesome creatures."

"But the bags have no scent. What keeps them out?" Juliana asked, fascinated by odd-shaped roots and strangely colored powders and fluids placed neatly about the room.

"Scentless to you, young lady. But not to insects. Works nearly as well as my potions to keep out field mice."

"I say, Mrs. Forbes, wherever did you learn about herbs and potions and the like?" Freddie asked, his face red and glowing from the heat, his neck cloth twisted under his left ear.

Lifting her head to a proud tilt, Mrs. Forbes's eyes touched them all one by one. "My grandmother was a Romany princess. She taught my mother and then me all the old ways."

"A gypsy princess! Did she teach you to read palms? Always wanted my palm read," Freddie declared with a wide grin.

"Palm reading is for gorgios at the fairs," scoffed Mrs. Forbes. "To tell the future ... yes ... sometimes. My grandmother had the eye. But not my mother."

Juliana glanced at Dominic and found him smiling that wonderful heart-stopping smile. "A tribe of gypsies camps on my grandfather's lands in Kent every spring. When I was young, I climbed down the creeper outside my bedroom window and went to the woods to listen to their music."

"Yes," Mrs. Forbes nodded slowly, her eyes resting thoughtfully upon Dominic. "Music is the gift of God to the gypsies. Robbie has the gift. After dinner tonight perhaps he will play for you in the garden."

"That sounds wonderful!" exclaimed Juliana. She had a long-standing fascination with gypsies after once sneaking off to a local fair with George and Will. They had proven unsatisfactory companions, however, for when she had wanted to enter the colorful tent where an old gypsy woman sat gazing into a crystal ball, they had dragged her back to the pony cart and driven home. "I look forward to hearing Robbie play," Juliana continued wistfully.

"There are dark circles under your eyes, miss," replied Mrs. Forbes. "I have brewed a new elixir for you, so you must rest today. That is what you need, rest and quiet, and that you shall have. Then tonight we shall see."

Fully rested after a long dreamless sleep in her bedroom, no doubt brought about by Mrs. Forbes's marvelous potion, Juliana sat at the window under the dormer. She looked out into the garden through which Lord Liscombe and the marquis were returning from their ride. They were apparently sharing a jest. When the marquis flung back his head, his thick golden hair gleamed in the sunlight, and Juliana thought him a handsome sight indeed. Laughter made him almost approachable. It was difficult to believe that he was the same autocratic lord who had tried to order young Ben and gone so far as to take over the fixing of her coach. She preferred him the way he had been today in Mrs. Forbes's kitchen and now, his face full of delight. Bringing the pink rose to her lips, she reveled again in its sweet scent. It was impossible not to feel the marquis's charm even though she had no personal interest in him whatsoever. When Sophia joined her at the window, she quickly concealed the rose.

Staring down at the two young men, Sophia sighed, "Do you suppose, Juliana, that the marquis might be what you are looking for?"

"Aunt Sophia!" Juliana cried, nearly tumbling off the window seat so great was her agitation. "Of course he doesn't fill my needs! He is neither middle-aged, nor I am sure, is he lonely and lacking female companionship."

Sophia smiled mischievously. "I am quite sure he does not!"

"Also, dear Aunt, he may very well already possess a marchioness."

"I had forgotten about that," replied her aunt, looking a little guilty, but she immediately brightened. "He doesn't behave like a married man. But we must discover his matrimonial status as soon as possible."

"Aunt Sophia, what has come over you!" Juliana felt curiously anxious about Sophia's newfound gaiety. Somehow Sophia appeared to be getting younger the farther away from Wentworth Park they traveled. She is only thirty-nine, Juliana suddenly remembered, not really old at all.

"Have I grown an extra nose, dear?" Sophia asked pleasantly, her special smile making her truly lovely.

"Oh, Aunt!" Juliana laughed, launching herself from the window seat to take Sophia's hands and plant a cheerful kiss on her cool cheek. "I was just realizing how young you really are. We should be looking for a husband for you."

Sophia smothered a smile. "Such nonsense. The marquis would not suit me at all." A strange look came over her features. "I am very pleased we decided to go to London. We must make the best of it." She slipped an arm around Juliana's shoulders, giving her a quick hug. "I'm famished. I can hardly wait to see what Mrs. Forbes has in store for us tonight."

Dinner, Aunt Sophia would have said, was an interesting combination of unexpected dishes. Certainly it was a vast improvement over parties at The Willows. When one dined with Sir Alfred and Lady Grenville, one always dined on mutton. Monotonous as it might be, it was often the only source of entertainment.

Juliana felt Aunt Sophia's burst of gaiety was catching. The air of excitement was so strong in the small parlor she could almost touch it. Freddie, seated to her left, took great pains to entertain and, indeed, his stories, no doubt carefully edited, about life in London caused both Juliana and her aunt to smile.

At just the right instant Dominic entered the conversation

with a witty aside that enhanced the tale and brought them all to laughter. He spoke with ease and knowledge on any number of subjects, encompassing politics, the late French wars, literature, and humorous *on-dits* concerning the beau monde.

Juliana studied him carefully, for although she tried not to admit it, he held an odd fascination for her. It was not only his arresting face and his athletic body, but his mind was a storehouse of delight that she was beginning to have an alarming eagerness to explore.

As though he felt her regard, Dominic turned to her, smiling, and Juliana's heart quickened. His fingers touched her hand. "Come, Juliana," he murmured softly, drawing her to her feet. "I believe your wish is about to be granted."

Startled and a little frightened that he could have read her thoughts, she stared at him for an instant before following his gaze to the doorway where Mrs. Forbes stood with Robbie, who held an ancient violin.

The night sky blazed with stars and the air was unseasonably warm for May. By moonlight Mrs. Forbes's garden was a fairyland of shadows and scents.

Sophia eschewed the heavy lavender-scented quilts Robbie spread upon the ground and sat on the stone bench beside Juliana. It seemed natural for Dominic to sit on the grass at Juliana's feet, his thick golden hair so close she would have only to reach out her hand to run her fingers through the curls.

Goodness, the lump on my head must have addled my brains, she told herself sternly. Folding her fingers tightly together, she looked up to where Robbie ran his bow tentatively over the strings of the violin. Soft notes filled the garden weaving a gentle serenity. She could hear Sophia sigh softly beside her, and Dominic leaned his head back against the edge of her bench. Suddenly the mood changed, great trills of notes enticed them to keep time to the lively music while Mrs. Forbes tapped her tambourine. Juliana could envision bare feet stamping and bright skirts twirling to the sparkling tune.

Then suddenly Robbie was singing and the violin became sweet, haunting strings. The theme of the music was earthly passion. The songs sprang from every country and every age of Romany wanderings. Songs eerie with the yearnings of long-forgotten lovers, with lost tears and remembered laughter. Songs that spoke directly to the heart.

She looked at Dominic. The moonlight defined his profile. Perhaps he felt her gaze, for he turned and rested his wide and solemn eyes upon her.

Drugged with the beauty of the music, she did not look away when she should have, but instead let the sweetness of the moment fill her with a warmth that ran like fire through her blood.

The last note faded into the darkness and Juliana, dragging her gaze from the marquis's face, looked hazily around her. Tears stood in Aunt Sophia's gray eyes. Freddie, looking very young, nibbled thoughtfully on a thumb while gazing at Robbie.

Juliana caught Mrs. Forbes's eyes from where she stood near her grandson's shoulder and felt that for some minutes she had been watching her. Her browned and work-worn hand suddenly touched Robbie's arm, and he lowered the violin to his side.

They all sat silent, faintly dazed, until Mrs. Forbes spoke. "It is late. Robbie will see you to your rooms now."

They rose in silence, the magic of the haunting melodies having bewitched them, and Sophia placed her hand on Freddie's arm, moving back into the inn.

Juliana lingered in the midst of Mrs. Forbes's garden, unwilling to let her feelings go. She felt as if she had just come awake after a long sleep. Life was different somehow. The world had moved forward without her. Taking this trip to London was the right choice. She'd lived in the past with memories and regrets for too long. It was time to begin anew.

When she made no move to follow the others, Dominic stepped closer to her and they were breathing the same air, perfumed by an exotic mingle of flowers. Moonlight bathed his face with gilt, and Juliana felt her bones had turned to liquid and were flowing away leaving her weightless. All of her excitement, her emotional response to the music, had to come from her decision to go forward with her life. It couldn't have anything to do with being alone in the moonlight with the marquis.

"The music was ... lovely, wasn't it?" she breathed, forcing herself to speak.

"Lovely ... yes," he whispered languorously, lifting her hand, turning it over to brush the inside of her wrist with his lips. He raised his eyes to her face and she met his look openly. What he saw there curled his mouth into a smile, and he twined their fingers together leading her deeper into the night garden.

Willingly she followed him into the shadows, captivated by the tenderness in his voice, the softness of his lips on her wrist, the gypsy music lingering at the edge of her consciousness. She could touch now the excitement she had felt earlier. It was here at her fingertips.

They turned a corner on the pathway and were before the brick wall that protected the little garden. Dominic stopped, turning her to him, his face starkly beautiful in the moonlight. Slowly he raised his hands, twining his fingers deeply into the curls resting on her shoulders, and whispered her name. "Juliana."

The rich timbre of his voice saying her name evoked a memory, a cherished memory of Will saying her name with that same longing. And with that memory came the desire to feel again those feelings that Will had awakened in her. But she knew these yearnings were different; she had changed and this man was not her beloved Will. The feelings he evoked were not of a comfortable secure love, but of a turbulent passion that could pull her over an edge into unknown depths of emotion. But it seemed right, a natural part of this night and this place to tilt her head back to gaze up at him. His eyes flashed sapphire lights, igniting the fires of excitement so they burned within her. A whisper of fear sent a chill down her arms. His hands settled on her shoulders, propelling her gently into the warmth of his embrace. Juliana knew she ought not to close her eyes, but she did anyway. She could feel his mouth hovering above hers, warming her lips, stroking them with his sweet, wine-scented breath before slowly they touched.

I shouldn't be doing this, her mind flashed a warning, but it had been too long since she had been kissed, so Juliana quieted that voice, pleading for just one more moment. One more moment to feel this strange delight. Her hands went up to his chest to feel the strong steady beat beneath his jacket. It quickened slightly when his lips pressed hers again, more urgently this time. Cool and dry, his searching lips taught her a lesson that had long been hidden from her.

"Juliana ... so soft, so perfect," that enchanting voice whispered. His finger gently caressed her cheek and she slowly opened her eyes.

It was not like Will at all. It was like no feeling Will had ever evoked, not even during his careful, gentle lovemaking. This man took possession with one kiss as sweet, gentle Will never had in their month of marriage.

The slamming of a door brought Juliana out of her daze. Light flashed along the path and a brisk step broke them apart.

"Your lordship?" Mrs. Forbes's voice shattered the spell. "Bring the young miss in. The night air will bring an inflammation of the lung. Hurry now."

Turning back the way they had come, Dominic's arm encircled her waist and she leaned against him following Mrs. Forbes's retreating back. The heady perfume of night-blooming jasmine overpowered all the other scents in the garden. The air was heavy with it, pressing against her. The path seemed uneven now, and she stumbled slightly, but was caught firmly in his strong arms.

She needed to say something to him, needed to understand what was happening, but was unsure of what she wanted to know. Nevertheless she tilted her head against her shoulder, whispering, "Dominic..."

He placed two fingers over her parted lips. "In the morning ... Juliana. We will talk in the morning."

Chapter 3

From her bedroom window Juliana saw the sun rise over Mrs. Forbes's garden wall, now such an ordinary rose brick, so unlike the enchanted bower of the night before. She had not closed her eyes all night. At one point, in the dark, chill hours, she had lit her bedside candle to search through her luggage until she found her jewel case. Taking out the locket containing Will's and Sir Timothy's pictures, she had placed it under her pillow. She wasn't quite sure why she had done that, perhaps because suddenly Wentworth Park and the life she had lived there seemed very far away.

She tried to blame these feelings on the excitement of the trip to London and the anticipation she felt. She tried to blame her sudden eagerness for life on the romantic atmosphere created by Robbie's violin. She tried to blame those moments of madness in the garden on the moonlight: any reason, any other reason than the marquis himself. But she could not deny that Dominic Crawford, Marquis of Aubrey, was the reason she had not slept. His fingers pressing hers, his arms enfolding her, his lips caressing hers, awakening a new joy, freeing a flood of emotion she had thought locked away forever. He had understood, she had seen it in his eyes. And when he had said they would talk in the morning, she knew he, like she, was unable to break the spell around them. That he, like she, needed time to consider the strange affinity between them.

Somewhere in the distance a cock crowed. Everyone would be awake soon. She would once again see the marquis. The thought both frightened and pleased her. Juliana was not sure which emotion was stronger.

The cock crowed and Dominic stretched languidly under

the down coverlet. Another sleepless night. But instead of the dreams of Culter Towers that left him drenched in sweat, or tossing in blinding fury, or full of painful longing for his father and what once had been, his dreams had brought a longing for her. At last a woman he might trust. A woman like the one woman he had carried in his soul since that night on the Peninsula when a soldier spent his dying moments painting word pictures of his young wife at home. In spite of the years of corruption or perhaps because of them, Dominic had cherished that vision and idealized that woman until she became the unattainable goddess all young men yearn for. But he was no longer a young man who believed in dreams. They had all died for him and Jules in one night at Culter Towers.

Juliana had for a moment wiped away the pain of that night. And she had offered him hope for the future. He had seen it in her eyes, reflecting the brilliance of the moon, softening under his touch. He had felt it, when her hands so shyly had crept to his chest, no coyness, but instead a wonder of recognition in their touch. For the first time the wall he had built around himself had not protected him; Juliana had touched his heart.

But the years of corruption had taught him to beware, and those years intervened now, warning him to go slow, to be sure. This morning he would see her again and perhaps the cold light of day would temper the hope coursing through him. Yes, carefulness was the tack.

Breakfast, anticipated so anxiously by Juliana and Dominic, passed in the same congenial fashion as the day before. The constraint that had made her fainthearted when she entered the small private parlor slowly disappeared as she listened to Freddie again complaining about Timmings's absence. How silly she had been to suffer through such a long, sleepless night! Dominic, too, was the same charming man who had rescued them two days ago.

He treated her with consideration and reserve, if she thought his eyes deepened when they looked at her, if she imagined the lines had softened around his mouth, then that was all a hum. After all, he was a great lord and had probably kissed many girls in the moonlight. Aunt Sophia had at least warned her about that. Nothing had changed except in Juliana's mind. Obviously the accident and Dominic in the garden had affected her more strongly than it should have. After all, she was not a miss suffering her first kiss in the moonlight either! She did not know what she had expected this morning, but it was not this pretense, so artfully done, that nothing had happened between them last night.

But perhaps he was right. It was only a kiss. She would never allow herself to acknowledge the truth. New and frightening emotions were now a part of her world, and they had been born in the marquis's arms.

Juliana determined to put this confusion behind her by staying well out of the marquis's path, until a sudden spring thunderstorm kept them all indoors after luncheon. When Sophia suggested they play a hand of whist, Freddie, grinning widely, hastily produced playing cards and placed four chairs around the small square table in the private parlor.

"You have found the way to Freddie's heart, Sophia," joked the marquis, looking at his friend with amusement. "If the London belles used your method, then perhaps one of them could bring him up to snuff."

"Bring him up to snuff?" Sophia inquired innocently. "Lord Liscombe is still unwed?"

"Good God, ma'am, I should say, indeed!" declared Freddie in horrified tones.

The marquis looked at Sophia's blank face in admiration. "I also share Freddie's sad plight," he murmured.

Sophia's dimple appeared and she had the grace to look slightly embarrassed.

Juliana was mortified. Her aunt had been uncharacteristically forward and Dominic obviously knew what was on her mind. Brooding in her own miserable confusion, Juliana had forgotten her aunt's interest in Dominic and his matrimonial status. She certainly hoped he was not conceited enough to imagine that his eligibility was of the slightest interest to her! Especially after allowing him to kiss her. Of course, with his looks women had no doubt been throwing themselves at his feet for years, so it could not be wondered at if he had a terribly swelled head.

His shapely head appeared to be just the right size and attached firmly to his broad shoulders; he played whist with the same sangfroid she had first noticed about him. Only in the garden last night had it seemed to slip.

Nevertheless Juliana found him an entertaining partner and an astute player, and she had played since she was old enough to count. Her father had often asked her to fill a table once he discovered she had a good memory and a quick mind.

She was blissfully unaware that Dominic was making a careful effort to please and to keep the atmosphere in the inn relaxed and informal.

Freddie, however, had not been fooled. Amused, he had taken Dominic aside earlier. "Dom, never seen the master rake at work in this style before. Surprised at the gentle tone of your flirtation. If I didn't know you better, think the lovely Juliana had caught your fancy."

Dominic had shrugged it off then, but truth to tell he didn't quite understand himself the reasons for his uncharacteristic behavior.

Glancing over the rim of his cards, he caught Juliana staring intently at her hand while her small white teeth raked her full lower lip. In the garden when he had succumbed to the need to take her in his arms and taste the sweetness of those lips, he had been unprepared for the depth of emotion she stirred in him. So stirred, he admitted ruefully, that he had retreated back behind his walls of defense. He had been told too many times for it to hold any meaning that his charm was lethal, but he sensed that Juliana had not fallen victim to it in the usual fashion. Careful, my lord marquis, he mused, you are dangerously close to falling victim to her charm. Looking at her lovely face, the soft cheeks slightly flushed with excitement, and having the dreary afternoon lightened by the musical, rippling sound of her laughter when she found the right card, caused Dominic, connoisseur of beautiful but heartless women, to want to believe that perhaps he had been wrong, that despite the past a woman could be trusted.

Juliana glanced up at exactly that moment, and the expression in Dominic's eyes caused her to cease thinking for an instant as if someone had doused her with ice-cold water. She was so bemused she did not notice the commotion coming from the hallway until the door burst open. Only then could she tear her gaze away from the marquis's face.

The loud argument in the hallway shattered their peace and privacy, when a corpulent woman, wearing a voluminous red cape glistening with raindrops, pushed open the door and disdainfully scanned the room. "I told you so, Charlotte! I just knew that was the Vane carriage in the Wainwright's yard as we passed!"

Sophia gasped and fell back in her chair. "Good God! It is Lady Grenville and Charlotte!"

Lady Grenville's protuberant eyes darted around the room taking in all of the occupants until coming to rest firmly on Sophia's face. "What is the meaning of this, Sophia?" Shifting her gaze to Juliana, she puffed her heaving bosom even higher. "And you! You should know better! A member of my own family alone in an inn parlor with these … these … men! Have you an explanation for this outrage?"

Dominic, resigned to the loss of this idyll, smiled quite naturally before stepping forward. "Ma'am, I am the Marquis of Aubrey. May I be of service?"

Lady Grenville's face turned an unhealthy crimson before she screeched at the top of her lungs. To everyone's shock, she cast herself into Dominic's arms. He staggered only slightly under her considerable weight.

"Dominic, my dear, dear boy!" she boomed only a bare inch below his right ear. His magnificent blue eyes flickered once as she continued to embrace him before tearing herself away to grasp the arm of the tall, slender, fair girl standing behind her. "Charlotte, come meet your cousin Dominic!"

Her flushed face beaming, Lady Grenville gave a breathy cry of delight when her daughter, in a spring muslin with a flounce of blond lace at the hem, walked forward. "I barely recognized you!" she continued loud enough for the postboy to hear. "You have changed so since we last met at Culter Towers."

Dominic's brows went up, but he gave no other sign of surprise, merely bowing over Charlotte's hand, saying, "How do you do, Miss Grenville. May I introduce Lord Freddie Liscombe." Smiling, he looked at Juliana and she moved to his side. "Of course, Juliana is known to you." Dominic glanced around at Sophia who seemed rooted to her chair. "Sophia, are you all right?" asked the marquis gravely.

"How could I not have seen it?" Aunt Sophia stood and stared at him. "You are the Duke of Culter's grandson!"

"Of course, he is dear Austin's grandson," Lady Grenville said, a haughty look descending upon her chubby features. "I am quite sure you have heard me mention their graces many times these past four years!"

"Many, many times," Aunt Sophia muttered, and Dominic's lips twitched appreciatively when she brushed pass him to place two warm kisses on both of Charlotte's pale cheeks.

Juliana stole a glance at the marquis. He endured a stilted conversation with Lady Grenville, whom he was assisting to a low couch beside the fireplace, when she admitted a slight faintness at discovering her dear cousin Dominic so unexpectedly.

Propping one broad shoulder against the wooden mantel, he apologized for not recognizing her, since he had only been an infant of nine months upon the occasion of her last visit to Culter towers.

He smiled across the small, cozy parlor at Juliana sharing the joke. She felt warmth flush her cheeks, but unconsciously she lifted her chin when she met a steely stare from beneath Lady Grenville's thin brows.

"I see you have already made the acquaintance of our neighbors," Lady Grenville said in a brittle voice. "Juliana is the widow of Will Grenville, the late Sir Timothy's only son." Twittering in a breathless little voice, her tight mouth twisted in a sly smile. "The Willows belongs to Sir Alfred and me now, you know."

Deep within him Dominic's heart gave one strong stroke

as if on an anvil. Will Grenville's bride? The woman he had idealized from all the stories he had heard around the camp fire. This was her, that picture of perfection that Will had drawn while he lay dying in Dominic's arms? It couldn't be! Jealousy rose like bile in his throat. She had belonged to someone else. Why had she led him to believe she was a Thatcher? If only he had known she was Will Grenville's bride, he never would have kissed her—never would have violated the memory of Will calling for his beloved Ju. The man Dominic had become did not deserve such a woman.

If she had not been so aware of him, Juliana would have missed the change that came over Dominic. One instant he was propped against the mantel, long legs braced apart, watching her with apparent delight, and a moment later those wonderful eyes somehow lacked their previous warmth and, although his expressive lips still smiled, there was a difference—the smile was distant and strained.

"My condolences, Juliana."

He spoke in a gentle voice that held a trace of something she couldn't quite recognize, but it made her reply terse.

"Thank you."

Freddie shook his head, a wrinkle creasing his brow. "Will Grenville ... I knew him on the Peninsula, remember Dominic? Nice young chap with the unruliest mop of ebony curls I've ever seen."

Juliana's eyes flew to Freddie's face. "You were on the Peninsula?"

"We both were. Dominic was a part of Wellington's family. General staff you know. Mentioned twice in the dispatches. I had no such luck, being sent home before Badajoz with a fever."

"Yes," Juliana nodded, the tightness in her throat causing her voice to break a little. "Will died at Badajoz six years ago."

Where was the teasing, affectionate consideration that Dominic had given her so freely and effortlessly since they first met? And something more that she refused to put a name to? He appeared like a man preoccupied with a longing to be elsewhere, but too well-bred to appear bored. It was not her imagination, for Freddie looked so decidedly uncomfortable he ran one finger around his high shirt collar, and Sophia's serene gray eyes held a look of curious concern.

"Come, Mama. Let us freshen ourselves," Charlotte suddenly spoke, moving to her mother's side.

Lady Grenville was totally unaware of the strange tensions in the room, for she opened her mouth to protest, but Charlotte got a firm grip on her arm, and with a cool nod to both gentlemen, led her protesting parent away.

"Did you see that!" Freddie breathed in an astonished voice. "Girl hasn't said a word since she walked in the door. Now she's ordering her mother about!"

"Charlotte is a young woman of few words," Sophia said calmly, her eyes still studying Dominic's stony profile. "But her timing is flawless."

Several hours later, the marquis steadied his grays as they sprang forward after a brief stop at the last tollgate on the London road. The twilight was gone and a strong breeze brought the smell of dirt and the damp chill of spring.

"It ain't that I'm not eager to get to town," continued Freddie, who had occupied himself ever since they left the Blue Boar in complaining about their abrupt departure. "I can't think what's come over you! Told the ladies we were staying and then you up and leave as soon as the Grenvilles arrive. Thought her ladyship would have an apoplexy when you said there was no need for us to stay as you knew she'd wish to convey Sophia and Juliana to London herself!"

Dominic grunted but said nothing more, his attention remaining firmly on the road. In fact, he had had very few words to say in the last several hours.

Not a man to be put off, Freddie glanced at him out of the corner of his eye. "Juliana is certainly a diamond of the first water. Didn't realize she was a Grenville. I thought she was a Thatcher like Sophia. Remember on the Peninsula how that young cavalry lieutenant, Will Grenville, talked about her and their land in Berkshire?" Freddie shook his head, smiling. "Brought a few tears to my eyes sometimes, remembering home. Glad I met her before she reached town. Lay you a wager she'll be all the rage within a fortnight!"

Dominic smiled, but it was strained, not in his usual way at all. "Yes ... I feel sure Juliana will take." His voice echoed the shock gripping him.

Freddie peered at him. "Devil!" he said with great feeling. "Forget about your preference."

"Which preference do you speak of?" asked Dominic with quiet cordiality. "My unexplainable preference for your questionable company, perhaps?"

"You prefer your women with experience. Safer I guess. But not widows. Can't understand that! Remember it struck us all as strange when the Duke of Cumberland stuck his spoon in the wall, you didn't give that delectable widow of his a second glance. Every man in the *ton* wanted her. She wanted you. And you not interested! Stands to reason Juliana isn't in your line. A dazzler, but fades besides the Duchess of Cumberland," said Freddie with brutal frankness.

Dominic was hardly aware of his friend's chatter, for the truth was finally penetrating through his shock. The warm, vibrant woman he had held in his arms was Juliana Grenville! He had thought the fates had played their last cruel trick on him, but he had been wrong. Oh, yes, he remembered Will and the stories that had brought tears to Freddie's eyes.

Dominic had been at the slaughter that was Badajoz. He had sat in the oozing mud, listening to the death groans of men spread across the battlefield, captivated by the over bright smile on Will's face as he had clasped Dominic's hand.

"Worst battle yet, but one good thing's come out of it. Think this wound will send me home to my Ju? Can't wait to see her red mop and take her down to fish again." He'd risen slightly on one elbow, so far gone he didn't even realize his legs had been shot away. "She's beautiful, Aubrey, yet daring. You should have seen her the day she outraced me to the pond and her horse balked, sending her head first into the stream. She rose with the water cascading down her gown and blushed to see me stare at her. God, she was beautiful." He had slipped back into Dominic's arms. "Ju, Ju, are you there?" Dominic's embrace tightened to give comfort, and Will smiled, the mist closing over his eyes.

Dominic had sat for long moments cradling Will, whose company had attacked the enemy's most heavily defended position, and their charge had helped swing the battle to the English side. But at too deep a price. With horror growing all around him, he had wondered how, so far from home in such a hellish death, Will could have died with the sweet vision of a woman his last thought.

Bright and shining in the dim recesses of his memory, he had kept an image of Will Grenville's young wife to combat the horror of war and the lingering agony of Culter towers. Only his half brother, Jules, knew the secrets they had vowed to bury along with their parents. In those moments when Dominic had felt his life was changed forever, he had demanded of Jules that neither of them ever marry.

Lately though, his grandfather had convinced Dominic that it was his duty to carry on the line. He had allowed himself to be convinced, for, tainted though he may be, his grandfather's blood also ran in his veins and that was worth preserving. He had supposed that someday he would find someone he could tolerate and who would be satisfied with only a crown of strawberry leaves, for he believed he had nothing else to give and was no longer fit for any woman who expected more. Juliana had destroyed that belief for a moment. But, of course, she would, she was Will's Ju. She could bring solace even amidst the horrors of war. To have at last come face-to-face with his elusive memory and know he must in no way reach out to her, was the greatest irony of his ill-fated life.

"Dominic, what the devil is ailing you? Do you agree or not?"

With an unpleasant twist to his firm mouth he finally glanced at his best friend. "Concerning my taste in women? How astute you have become, Freddie. My congratulations."

Freddie shrugged, completely ignoring his sarcasm. "I like widows myself, they know what to say to a man. Not like those simpering misses straight out of the schoolroom, like that Charlotte Grenville."

"That Charlotte Grenville, I very much fear, is the distant relative my grandmother has been hinting would make me an unexceptional marchioness."

"Thinking of falling into parson's mousetrap are you, Dom?" asked Freddie with a worried glance.

For a fleeting instant a picture of Juliana rose in his mind. "No!"

"Wouldn't want to go against your grandmother, the duchess, if it was me. Forceful woman your grandmother. And your grandfather!" Freddie shook his head, shifting restlessly upon the curricle seat. "He's a match for anyone! Even heard Prinny say he could make him feel like a schoolboy again."

"Ah, but I have advantages you and the Prince don't possess, Freddie," Dominic drawled. "Their graces and I are very much alike."

The shutters on Mrs. Forbes's wide kitchen windows were flung back and sunshine left large warm patches upon the stone floor. Sophia placed the last jar of elixir in the willow basket Robbie had provided her with this morning. She turned to Mrs. Forbes, who was sitting before the crackling fire drinking some hot potion from a cup.

"Thank you so much," Sophia said, her eyes drifting about the kitchen, touching on exotically shaped roots and herbs hung tidily from the ceiling beams, remembering the laughter they had all shared brewing gypsy potions. "We have enjoyed ourselves so here. I shall not forget our visit."

"I know you will never forget this place, Sophia. It was the beginning of all your tomorrows," said Mrs. Forbes, granddaughter of a Romany princess.

Surprise took Sophia to the fireplace to stand before Mrs. Forbes. Clearly seen in the merciless sunlight, her strong proud features were alert and so were her shrewd dark eyes, in spite of the lines deeply etched into her face revealing great age.

Sophia met her gaze calmly and smiled. "Are you trying to tell me something? I noticed you did not fully answer Freddie's question concerning fortune-telling. You simply said your mother did not have the eye ... I would almost believe you do possess it."

Mrs. Forbes' wrinkles deepened. "Ha! You are a practical woman. You do not believe in the eye, so I will only tell you your real reason for going to London will prosper richer than your brightest dreams. The thread was spun long ago and now you pick it up once again."

Sophia no longer smiled as a chill played across her skin. There was such a ring of sureness in Mrs. Forbes's voice that Sophia almost believed the future was hers to see. "I do not understand," she murmured.

"Of course you do not!" retorted Mrs. Forbes. "You are not meant to. Hurry along now, the others are waiting for you. Your niece will be along shortly."

Juliana waited until the coachman was attempting to help Lady Grenville into the carriage, with the aid of Charlotte and Aunt Sophia, before she made her way to Mrs. Forbes's kitchen. She found her in the walled garden pruning the rose bush from which Dominic had plucked her bloom.

Mrs. Forbes looked up when Juliana approached. "I've been waiting for you, young miss. Knew you would come to say farewell."

Leaning over, Juliana brushed the weathered brown cheek with her lips. "You have been so kind to us. I shall never forget this place. Or you."

Mrs. Forbes's face changed and a ghost of a smile touched her mouth. "Come, Juliana, give me your hand," she commanded.

Uncertain, Juliana hesitated before slowly holding out her right hand. It lay on Mrs. Forbes's thin palm, pink and white and young against the dark aged skin.

A pain in her chest suddenly made Juliana aware that she was holding her breath, and she let it out carefully before Mrs.

SHERRILL BODINE

Forbes lifted her eyes. Juliana was captured in the older woman's dark gaze and stood absolutely still.

"There are two things you want, Juliana. One you know well. The other you are just discovering. One you shall never have, nor is its loss worth your sorrow. The other shall be yours, although the road twists and turns, bringing pain and tears. Go with your feelings ... here..." She placed her left palm over Juliana's heart. "Not with the rules you know well. And all will be as it should be."

A large tear ran down Juliana's cheek. At the same moment, Mrs. Forbes abruptly covered the palm with its fingers and returned the folded hand to its owner. "Be happy. You now have the key."

Minutes later Juliana climbed into Lady Grenville's newly painted traveling coach. It was over: their strangely unsettling, strangely exciting time at the Blue Boar Inn. There would be no more adventures on her journey. She would reach London, find a comfortable husband, and establish her brother firmly in the bosom of the *ton*. That was what she wanted, the plan she and Aunt Sophia had devised. But what else did she desire?

Instantly her thoughts flew to the two sleepless nights she had spent filled with visions of the Marquis of Aubrey. Those moments they had spent in Mrs. Forbes's garden almost seemed like a dream now, a dream spun by the magic of Robbie's Romany music. A dream that must be put behind her. The marquis had occupied too many of her thoughts already. She was behaving like the veriest peagoose! It was simply a kiss. Nothing more.

Incurably honest with herself, Juliana closed her eyes, brushing her fingers lightly over her brow before opening her lids wide again. It had been like no embrace she had ever known, she finally admitted. The Marquis of Aubrey drew her to him in a way she had never imagined possible. In Mrs. Forbes's cozy parlor she had thought he also sensed this thing between them, that in some way he was reaching out to her. But the next instant he had closed himself away from her as surely as if a door had clicked shut between them.

Forcing herself not to think any longer about the marquis,

50

she glanced at her aunt, who appeared to be lost in her own thoughts, her eyes holding a strange brightness. So Juliana turned to look out onto the countryside. Soon they would be in London. Their future lay there. It would be just as she wished, she felt sure, for she was determined the plan would succeed. But, nonetheless, she could not keep Mrs. Forbes's words out of her mind.

Chapter 4

ROME

Jules Devereaux, Comte de Saville, intended only to pause for one last glance into the bedroom, but the seductive golden beauty of the woman clearly discernable behind the gossamer hangings of silk drew him closer. She looked like a goddess, long silken limbs, skin of creamy alabaster, dark thick lashes laying like open fans above her sleep-blushed cheekbones, and crimson velvet lips.

On impulse, with two long fingers he pushed back the netting to slip noiselessly onto the ornately carved wooden bed that held his mistress. She stirred him more than he had thought possible so few hours after their long night of love, so he rested his hands on the pillow beside her shoulders and leaned forward to touch her mouth with his own. He felt her lips part hungrily beneath his deepening kiss.

"Jules…" breathed Contessa Marietta Louisa Primavetta, opening heavy brown eyes, which widened when they met his gaze. "What is the hour, Cara?"

"It is nearly dawn. My ship leaves on the tide."

She cupped his cheeks with her palms, pulling him down to her. Her tongue flicked across his straight mouth curving it into a smile and finally he surrendered, sighing, and rested his head against her breasts. "You are unusually … eager … tonight, my love. I find it delightful, of course," he mused. "But unlike you."

"You have never left me for months before, Jules," she whispered, threading her fingers through his straight dark hair. "Must you truly return to dreary London for that insipid Season?"

Reluctantly leaving the soft fragrance of her body, Jules

straightened, taking both her hands between his. "I must go. The time is right for me to repay my brother for the past."

Her gaze narrowing, she freed one hand to touch the black patch he wore over his left eye. "Your younger brother, the Marquis of Aubrey, is it not? Did he have anything to do with the loss of your sight?"

"Sweet, allow me my secrets." He pressed kisses into her open palms. "It was my mysterious past and my patch ... you thought me a pirate, remember? ... that first attracted you to me."

"But that was seven years ago. And I know little more about your past now than I did then," replied Marietta candidly. Tilting her head back, she smiled into his face. "You have not been back to England since we met. I know your half brother is your only relative. Do you miss this loved one, Cara?"

Gently he lowered her hands to the covers and rose from the bed. He hesitated a moment, studying her, before reaching down to caress the curve of her cheek with his thumb. "Love for my brother. Yes. Once. But that does not call me back to England. It is something quite different. Something that must be settled between Dominic and me ... at last."

LONDON

Wentworth House seemed small after the vastness of the Park, but Juliana rather liked the cozy front parlor. Her father had decorated it in her favorite colors of rose, blue, and cream only a few months prior to his unexpected demise from an inflammation of the lungs brought about by his stubborn refusal to leave the hunting field during a thunderstorm. It was difficult to believe that two long years had passed, for the holland covers removed from all the furnishings before their arrival, had insured that the colors remained true and everything was dusted and polished to a fine sheen just as if her father himself was in residence continually.

A small fire, for cheer rather than warmth, burned in the grate of the carved marble fireplace before which she sat with an unopened volume of Lord Byron's poems on her lap. Across the room Sophia lay stretched out upon the sofa. A soft snore parted her lips.

Juliana smiled. Perhaps a nap was just what she needed herself. She wasn't sleeping well. She had told her aunt it was the strange bed, but when she was completely honest with herself, she knew that was not true. Dreams disturbed her slumber. Dreams of the Marquis of Aubrey smiling at her as he had in the walled garden when he presented her with the rose. Dreams of him again bending over her hand and pressing his lips to the pulse beating in her wrist. Dreams of a stolen moment, his tender kiss. Dreams that assumed nightmare quality when he raised his head to look at her and she found that his wonderful face had changed into a hard, angry mask that chilled her. It was that coldness that always awakened her, for she'd find her bedclothes tossed aside as if in her restlessness she had pushed and kicked them away. Dominic Crawford, Marquis of Aubrey, why did he haunt her?

Abruptly the parlor doors were flung open by Smithers, wearing his habitually sour expression.

"The Marquis of Aubrey and Lord Freddie Liscombe!" he announced in a booming voice, which caused Sophia to jump, her eyelids flying open, and her hands fluttering to her white lace cap which was sadly askew.

The object of Juliana's thoughts stood seemingly relaxed, smiling with cool civility, framed like a Della Robbia angel within the wide rectangle of the parlor door. He looked magnificent. The cut of his deep blue morning coat displayed to perfection the breath of his splendid shoulders, and its color set off the uniquely rich gold of his hair.

She gazed at him, feeling the tiniest bit giddy, much as she had on her eighteenth birthday when she had partaken of four glasses of champagne. She freely admitted that the lump on her head, sustained in the carriage accident, had had nothing to do with her state of mind at the inn; she was very strangely affected by this gentleman she barely knew, and who had proven by his unconventional behavior that he might not be worthy of her friendship. She found she was holding her breath in anticipation.

His behavior was disappointingly conventional this morning. He greeted Sophia warmly, but only raised Juliana's fingers toward his lips, managing to miss contact entirely. Dominic stepped back for Freddie to greet her in a like manner, except the pleasant smile that brightened his brown eyes was a great deal warmer than the marquis's, and his lips pressed gently against her fingers.

"How kind of you both to call. Please be seated." Sophia said cordially, patting the low cream sofa upon which she was reclining, and motioning Freddie to the rose velvet bench beside Juliana.

"How do you like London, Juliana?" Freddie asked eagerly, sitting forward on the bench at such an angle that she feared he would tumble over.

She smiled easily, "London is splendid, Lord Liscombe. We are quite looking forward to the Season."

"It can be tedious, Juliana. Of course, all depends on your expectations," Dominic drawled. "I hope it comes up to yours, ma'am."

Juliana glanced away from Freddie's intent face to where Dominic sat on the sofa, one hand playing idly with his quizzing glass. The mouth she remembered as perfect, soft, and persuasive in the garden was curled into a hard derisive smile. All those tender memories tightened inside her, a small rose of perfection closing against the onslaught of night. Obviously he had taken a dislike of her, for how else could she explain this odd behavior? But she was not such a poor-spirited creature that she would allow him to see how much it disturbed her.

Raising her chin, she looked at him with what she hoped was a withering glance, but immediately thought better of it. Instead she deliberately widened her eyes and fluttered her lashes, a simpering miss straight out of the schoolroom awed by the honor he did them by his morning call. "I am sure it will not be a disappointment, my lord," she replied in what she knew was a languid tone. "It is all a shocking squeeze, of course, but it is delightful to have such new friends as Lord Liscombe and you, my lord marquis." If Dominic was determined to be rude and boorish, she would show him that she could not be so easily overset. How foolish she was to have even a flicker of regard for him. He was nothing but a conceited flirt! The only explanation for his behavior was that he had found it amusing to dazzle them with his charm at the Blue Boar, thereby adding her to his long list of conquests. And, now that they were in London he no longer chose to so honor them. Well, she for one, would not be so shabbily used!

The marquis's lips twitched in apparent amusement at her schooled expression of demure delight, but Aunt Sophia was not so affected. She eyed Juliana doubtfully for a moment before the dimple hovered beside her mouth. Then turning to the marquis, she deftly changed the subject. "Is Lord Rodney in town, Dominic?"

His eyes lightened as surprise flitted across his face. "Know my uncle do you, Sophia? Shouldn't admit it, my dear. He's the worst reprobate in the *ton*. The duchess has quite washed her hands of the old boy."

Aunt Sophia raised her eyebrows in lively curiosity. "Really, Dominic? How intriguing! He sounds more fascinating than he was twenty years ago when I knew him. I look forward to renewing our acquaintance."

The Marquis of Aubrey stretched his arm lazily across the back of the sofa. "I believe you will have the pleasure of meeting him again at Miss Grenville's ball Friday next."

Sophia smiled. "I would hardly expect to find the worst reprobate in the *ton* at a come-out ball."

"Quite so, ma'am," he laughed softly. "However, my grandmother has decreed that my uncle and I both attend as Lady Grenville is in some way connected with the family."

"I say, that was quite a coincidence Dominic running into his cousins at the Blue Boar," Freddie chuckled. "Did Mrs. Forbes mix any elixir for her ladyship?"

Biting her lip, Juliana met Sophia's bright eyes before her aunt replied, "Yes, a potion to curtail her appetite."

"Does it work?" Freddie questioned eagerly. "My mother

could use it. She's drinking vinegar now because Byron says that's how he keeps thin. Damn silly if you ask me!"

Nodding her head, Aunt Sophia cast him an understanding glance. "So right, Freddie. Vinegar indeed! But I'm quite sure Mrs. Forbes's potion would work. Didn't everything else? However, Lady Grenville chose to leave it behind, saying it was such an obnoxious mixture she wouldn't feed it to a sow."

"Oh, I say, I hope Mrs. Forbes's feelings weren't hurt." Such a heavy crease appeared in Freddie's forehead, Juliana patted his hand.

"Don't worry. Aunt Sophia put it with our own herb potions and brought it with us. She thought it might come in handy someday."

"And so it might," commented her Aunt. "Oh, thank you, Smithers. You may place the tea tray here in front of me. I shall pour."

Certainly Dominic had been carefully watching a clock tick away the minutes because after one cup of tea and exactly the correct span of elapsed time for a morning call, he rose leisurely from the sofa and bent over Sophia, lightly kissing her fingers. "I trust we will meet again at the Grenville ball and that Uncle Rodney isn't a disappointment to you."

"Of course, Dominic, I look forward to seeing you both there," Sophia returned serenely. "I am sure Juliana shall also be happy to see you."

Without meeting her eyes, something he had studiously avoided all morning, Dominic sketched a neat bow at Juliana before casting a disgusted look at Lord Liscombe. Much to Juliana's embarrassment, Freddie was leaning forward on the bench earnestly studying her profile. "Stop making such a cake of yourself, Freddie! It's time to take our leave."

"Gammon!" said Freddie, looking not a whit displeased at this reading of his behavior. "Just want to invite Juliana to drive in the park tomorrow. Had to wait until you finished discussing your family tree. Poor Rod! He's not the worst reprobate in the *ton*, Old Cripplegate is and you know it! Quite fond of Rod myself and I'm sure Sophia and Juliana will be, too!"

Juliana met the diamond brightness of Dominic's eyes at last in a brief instant of shared amusement and was more confused than ever. Drat the man! His behavior was totally incomprehensible. One moment he looked at her with an aloof coldness that bordered on dislike, and the next she saw in his eyes a warmth that was quite pleasant, indeed.

For some reason she did not understand he was no longer the same man who had walked with her in Mrs. Forbes's garden and sat under the stars spellbound by Robbie's music. Why had he changed? Had she somehow offended him? How? And what could she do to rectify her error? She would like him to be a friend, for London was his world, not hers, and she was a bit frightened of it. She had lived too long in the tranquility of Wentworth Park. She felt she had been drifting aimlessly for the last six years and now the hustle and bustle of the city was quickening her blood, tingling her nerves, opening her eyes again to the world.

"Juliana, Freddie is waiting for an answer," her aunt firmly reminded her.

How long had she been woolgathering? Hot with embarrassment, she smiled her gentlest smile, the one she had perfected for Reverend Potts whenever she fell asleep during one of his sermons, and turned her eyes to Freddie's expectant face.

"I would be most happy to drive with you tomorrow. I quite look forward to it!"

"I'm honored, Juliana," Freddie bowed, his wide cheeks flushed with pleasure.

For once Dominic's expression was not difficult for Juliana to interpret. He was looking at her like a farmer mulling over what to do about the fox in his fowl yard. It would have been pleasant to match his stare with a cold one of her own, but she somehow maintained her fixed smile of pleasure until the door clicked shut behind them.

Biting her lip, she twirled away, pacing restlessly from the carved mantel to the blue velvet hung windows, to the small, round gilt mirror over the rosewood table. She stared at her reflection. She had been told she was beautiful, but all she saw in the mirror were green eyes in a sometimes too pale face, a nose a bit short for real beauty, and a mouth with a full lower lip. Pulling thick auburn curls first one way and then another, she attempted to change that image but was not pleased with the results.

Sophia subjected Juliana's back and reflection to a critical survey. "You really are quite beautiful, my dear. There really is no need for concern."

Juliana gave her a warm smile. "Thank you, love. I shall allow you to flatter me, but...," she frowned, "but I believe improvements could be made!"

Marching to the bellpull, she gave it a strong tug. Almost immediately Smithers appeared in the doorway. He did not look pleased, but then Juliana had found he never did.

"You require my services, ma'am?" he asked in sepulchral tones.

Aunt Sophia rolled her eyes looking to Juliana. Taking a stance before the fireplace, Juliana clasped her hands tightly in front of her.

"Smithers, I need your help," she said firmly. "My aunt and I wish to cut a dash at Miss Charlotte's ball, but we need advice. Who should gown us and dress our hair?" She gave him her most charmingly rueful grin. "Can you help us, Smithers? My Father always told me you were up to every rig and row in town."

Smithers's sour expression did not alter in the slightest. "As to that, Miss Juliana, I cannot say. However, I have been informed that Monsieur Henri is a genius with a coiffure. I have likewise been informed that Madame Bretin on Bond Street is the finest modiste in London." He bowed deeply. "I shall see to it, Ma'am."

Only after the door shut behind Smithers tall black-clad figure did Juliana allow herself a heartfelt sigh of relief.

"My dear, you were superb!" Sophia laughed. "I have always been in awe of Smithers, although...," she shrugged, "I can't imagine why, because he looks exactly like your late father's favorite hound Claudius. Have you ever noticed the resemblance?"

"Aunt Sophia, please! How can you say such things about Smithers? He shall fix us up all right and tight. Father depended upon him utterly. And in this instance I must do so, too, for I have no idea how to go on myself."

"Is this part of your campaign to find your lonely widower, my dear?" asked her aunt with a decided sparkle in her gray eyes.

A face flashed into Juliana's thoughts, but it had not the slightest resemblance to an aging widower. Why should she wish to impress him? Naturally, it was only her Vane family pride that made her wish to look her best; it had absolutely nothing to do with an absurd wish to once again see blatant admiration in a pair of magnificent blue eyes.

Juliana smiled with pleasure up into Freddie's round, open face. They had a perfect afternoon for a ride in the park.

Eyeing her in appreciation, Freddie's mouth curved into a wide grin when he helped her into his shining black curricle.

"You'll turn heads today, Juliana. You're in great looks," he complimented.

"Thank you," she replied softly, rather pleased herself with her dark green velvet pelisse and matching hat with its curled beige ostrich plume. She had kept Freddie waiting a fashionable twenty minutes while she took great care with her toilette. One never knew whom one might meet on a drive, she had said pertly to her aunt when quizzed about her uncharacteristic fussing. Settling back with a sigh, she turned a serene countenance to her companion. She was quite looking forward to this outing.

A strong spring breeze lifted Juliana's curled ostrich plume tickling her cheek. Laughing, she flicked it back into place, gazing once again in awe at the bustling knots of shoppers and hawkers on the streets of London. She thought she would never become accustomed to its crowded condition. The air was not the sweet, clean scent of Wentworth Park, rather a heavy acid smell, yet for some reason it filled Juliana with new energy.

They entered through the high stone gateway of Hyde Park and immediately joined the mass of barouches, phaetons, dashing curricles, beautiful horses with equally impressive riders, and old-fashioned landaus carrying the dowagers and young misses of the *ton* on Rotten Row.

Juliana had married Will without having a Season, but Freddie was well-known and apparently quite a favorite, for they were greeted on all sides and often stopped so that she could be introduced. Juliana feared she would never recall all her new acquaintances.

They had just left a plump, merry matron whom Freddie had introduced as Lady Jersey when, in a sonorous whisper, he informed her that Sally Jersey was one of the patrons of Almacks, that great bastion of the *ton*.

"No need to worry though," Freddie told her confidently. "Old harridan is a bosom friend of my mother's. Put a good word in for you with the old girl."

"Freddie! I'm sure Lady Jersey wouldn't enjoy being referred to as a harridan or as the old girl!" admonished Juliana with gentle firmness, much as she had done for years to George whenever he had forgotten his manners.

Lord Liscombe grinned. "You called me Freddie. About time! You're a very comfortable female to be around, Juliana."

She couldn't but laugh at his glowing face. "Why thank you … Freddie. You're very comfortable, too. You remind me of my brother George."

"Not sure I'm flattered that I remind you of your brother," Lord Liscombe said wistfully, gazing at her with wide, sorrowful eyes, his grin fading. "Not surprised though. Always happens when I'm with Dominic; no one notices me."

"The marquis! I have not given him a thought," Juliana snapped. "It is a great compliment to remind me of George," she added kindly.

Once again Freddie's grin widened. "Accept the compliment, Juliana. Glad to hear you ain't smitten with Dominic. Knew you were full of good sense! The way you handled yourself when you had the carriage accident, stands to reason you wouldn't fall at Dominic's feet like most women."

Deep within her Juliana felt her spirits plunge. "I was

under the impression that the marquis was your friend," Juliana responded quietly.

"Dom's been my best friend since we were in short pants! Don't mean I'm blind to his ways. Not his fault, I don't suppose, that the loveliest of the *ton* throw themselves at him. Should know better after all these years. All he does is raise their expectations and dash them when he becomes bored."

"It sounds as though the marquis is a rake," Juliana said, raising her chin.

Freddie cast a worried glance at her and encountered her arctic glare. "Dash it, you're right. Talking to you like my own sister. Shouldn't be talking to you like this about Dominic. He's a great gun, truly! The best horseman and finest swordsman in the whole *ton*. Bright too, so clever sometimes can't even fathom what he's talking about. Hard to read with the ladies, that's all."

"Don't concern yourself Freddie. I shall not repeat our conversation," she assured him with dignity.

Looking away from Freddie's worried face, she saw for the first time the Marquis of Aubrey riding toward them with the most dashing and beautiful lady she had ever encountered. As she watched, the vision turned her head to speak to Dominic, revealing a perfect profile with a sweep of raven black hair caught up under a fetching red hat à la Hussar set at a jaunty angle. Her red velvet riding habit with its black frogging and braid trim showed off her creamy complexion and her dark, slightly slanted eyes. They were indeed a striking couple, the golden marquis and this raven-haired beauty.

Dominic by moonlight had been stunning: the perfect angles of his face, the clear true tones of his skin, hair and eyes, the grace of his athletic, finely muscular body. Yet by the blaze of this afternoon's sun, he shone even more brilliantly, searching sunbeams turning his thick hair every shade of gold from citrine to amber.

Freddie followed the direction of her gaze. "That's Lady Dora Stanwood. The Earl of North's daughter and Dominic's latest flirt."

"They make a stunning couple," she murmured, unable to

drag her eyes away from them.

Freddie shrugged. "Dora thinks so. She's wild to a fault and the most determined yet to snare him. Doubt she'll do it though. Bets are on at White's that she won't bring him up to snuff. Her family wants her to have a crown of strawberry leaves, but they don't particularly want her to be Dominic's duchess." Flicking a side glance at her, Freddie coughed before adding, "His reputation you know."

By this time the marquis had spotted them, and the pair turned their horses, picking their way through the throng. The strong breeze which had teased Juliana's plume had also disordered Dominic's hair so that a heavy gold curl fell close to the tips of his thick lashes. There was nothing in his expression to try to interpret at this meeting. His perfect face was perfectly blank. "Good afternoon, Mrs. Grenville," he said smoothly. "I don't believe you've met Lady Dora Stanwood." Glancing at his partner a slow smile curled his lips. "Mrs. Grenville has just arrived for the Season."

"How do you do," Lady Dora said in a soft, highly refined voice. "I hope you will find London to your liking."

"Thank you. I feel sure I will," replied Juliana, deciding that Lady Dora's beauty had a cold perfection about it that she could not like.

Taking exception to a passing carriage, Dora's mare fidgeted slightly, rearing its head. With a nod and a cool smile her ladyship moved off. Dominic followed after the briefest of farewells. Juliana couldn't help looking behind her as the marquis and Lady Stanwood threaded their way carefully through riders and carriages until Freddie's voice brought her back to her surroundings.

"Wonderful stallion of Dominic's. Arabian you know."

"Yes. I was just admiring it," she said innocently, turning to look at him. "I'd love to ride the animal myself."

"Oh, I say! No chance of that!" he laughed. "No one rides Bucephalus but Dominic." For a moment he studied her. "Do you enjoy riding?"

"Oh, yes! I rode every day at home in Wentworth Park. My

father had me in the saddle before I could walk."

"Don't keep a stable in town myself, but Dominic does. Sure he'd be happy to find a proper mount for you. I'll speak to him if you'd like."

Juliana felt a ripple of excitement at the idea of riding beside the marquis, for she knew that at least in this she was his equal, but quickly pushed the thought away. "Thank you, but no. My aunt and I shall be quite busy getting settled in and preparing for Charlotte's ball."

"Hope you'll save me a dance," Freddie grinned. "Perhaps even the first one."

"Of course, Freddie. It is yours!"

Nodding, he returned his attention to his horses, guiding them carefully through the mass of traffic.

Juliana was pleased that for the moment she did not have to make conversation, for her mind was too busy with thoughts of the Marquis of Aubrey: remembering being held against his hard, muscular chest in the fleeting moments she had regained consciousness in his arms, the feel of his lips on her wrist pulse, the way he had looked at her when Robbie sang in the garden, the surprising emotion he awakened in her at the moment of a stolen kiss, the tenderness in his eyes in Mrs. Forbes's parlor before Lady Grenville arrived, and the way now he seemed to only look through her. Why did it bother her so? Freddie had told her Dominic was in the habit of dropping damsels the instant they bored him. That must be it! The answer to the puzzle of Dominic's behavior was quite simple; she had bored him. A fierce jolt of hurt moved through her body. A heartbeat later an equally fierce wish to have the Marquis of Aubrey groveling at her feet for some crumb of attention, which she denied him, rose deliciously to her mind. She knew such thoughts were not worthy of her, but never before had she been snubbed, however politely, by a gentleman and she found she did not care for it. Especially Dominic. Especially after the Blue Boar Inn. There had been something between them which she refused to treat lightly, even as she tried to push it out of her mind.

She would acknowledge that she had been attracted to him,

and now wished him to feel the same way. He had once, she knew, for she had seen it in his eyes in the garden and across the card table at the Blue Boar. Juliana did not know how she would do it, but that look would be there again. And as soon as it was, she would ... she would ... she wasn't quite sure what she would do.

The late afternoon sunshine pierced the windows of Wentworth House checkering the rose carpeting of the lady's salon where Aunt Sophia sat when Juliana returned from her drive.

"My dear, your plan has suffered a serious setback!"

Stopping in her tracks, a hot flush washed over Juliana. "How did you know?" she blurted out, for she was so consumed with her plans for the marquis that she was sure her aunt, who had an uncanny way of ferreting out the truth, had seen through her immediately. She dropped down upon the sofa. "I know it isn't worthy of me. I was sure you wouldn't approve."

Sophia raised her eyebrows. "Did you use your parasol?" she asked sharply, touching Juliana's flushed face. "Just as I suspected! You have a fever. You must go to bed at once."

"No, no, Aunt! I am quite well. Truly." Shaking her head, she cupped her warm cheeks with her palms, the wish to justify her intentions toward the marquis warring with a strong conviction that she should lay open her troubled spirit to her aunt. It took her a moment to decide which course she would take. "I have no fever. I cannot believe you could possibly know anything about my plan at this early date," she said defensively.

"Early date! We worked on this scheme for three months before we told George we were coming to London to find you a husband." Waving a letter underneath Juliana's nose she nearly shouted, "Now he is not coming!"

"The plan. Why didn't you say so in the first place?" she replied quickly, snatching the letter from her aunt's fingers.

"What other plan could I be speaking about? Are we not here for the sole purpose of luring your brother from his chores?"

From the interested look on Sophia's face Juliana feared

the wrong suspicion might be taking root in her fertile mind. Forcing a light laugh Juliana read George's sprawled writing. "He says that he is still coming and will only be a few days delayed." Glancing at her aunt, Juliana shrugged. "I see no need for concern." Allowing the sheet of paper to drift to Sophia's lap, Juliana rose from the sofa absently smoothing out the folds of her skirt.

"I felt sure you would be upset," Sophia said indignantly, then stopped, looking up at her with sudden understanding. "Does this mean you have changed your mind?"

Smiling ruefully, Juliana realized that Dominic had done what she had feared: caused her to stray from her purpose. But only briefly. As soon as she accomplished her admittedly unworthy goal, she would turn her back on him and continue with her plan to set her brother on the road to acquiring some town bronze and find for herself a comfortable widower so that when George did finally marry, he would not need to be concerned about his widowed sister.

"Yes," she said, lifting her chin with determination. "I believe, for the moment there is no hurry in finding my widower. We will simply enjoy the Season." Thankful to have decided at last what strategy she would follow, Juliana moved toward the parlor door only to be brought up short by her aunt.

"By the way, Smithers has arranged for us to visit Madame Bretin's on Bond Street tomorrow. Shall we still keep the appointment?"

"Of course. It is essential to my plan," Juliana sniffed before marching out of the room.

The instant the door clicked shut behind her, Sophia fell back upon the pillows, her delighted laughter filling the room. "At last! And now, Juliana my love, I can carry out my plan for you!"

Chapter 5

Smithers had outdone himself. When Sophia and Juliana arrived in Bond Street, Madame Bretin's shop was shuttered and a small card reading "By Appointment Only" was affixed to the door. Madame herself ushered them in with much ceremony, stating that she was delighted to be entirely at their service and able to devote herself to their special needs.

Juliana was slightly taken aback by this ingratiating behavior, but Sophia seemed to take it as their due. So Juliana unconcernedly moved to the tables laden with materials in every color of the rainbow and searched the shelves stacked with bolts of sheer muslins, linens, and batistes. Madame Bretin, much to Juliana's dismay, peered at her intently, watching her every movement as she seemingly assessed her figure. Finally, as if satisfied, Madame whirled briskly, urging them to the back of the shop, down a short hallway into a large room hung completely about with tall mirrors.

Bringing out a chair, she motioned Sophia to sit down. She turned to Juliana and without preamble asked her to remove her dress for the measurements. Juliana looked at her aunt for guidance, but Sophia smiled complacently and nodded her head in encouragement.

The couturiere was most exacting with her tape while she kept up a steady flow of compliments concerning Juliana's trim waist, full bosom, and long line of leg for one as petite as she.

Flushing with embarrassment, Juliana met the amused eyes of her aunt in the mirror, then quickly glanced away, biting her lip. She might have been so undignified as to chuckle at Madame's fulsome compliments if the modiste hadn't suddenly straightened from measuring Juliana's hips to peer intently into her eyes.

"A light spring green in silk for afternoon wear. A must!"

Fascinated, Juliana stood and watched Madame Bretin hold up swatches of materials in various colors against her skin, discarding some and exclaiming over others. She had to admit the couturiere's sense of color was outstanding. When Madame unfurled a bolt of French turquoise silk to drape about Juliana's body, she knew she had found exactly what she had envisioned for Charlotte's come-out ball.

Sophia settled into her chair, satisfied at last that her goal to establish Juliana in the *ton*, and find the right man for her, was well on the way to being achieved. No man, duke or earl, would be able to resist Juliana when she appeared in all this finery.

Silks so fine they could be pulled through a wedding ring, rich brocades, soft velvets, muslins, voiles, and heavy satins piled up at her feet.

"We are fortunate that dreadful war is over. These are the finest fabrics in all of Europe," Madame Bretin insisted.

Morning dresses, walking costumes, riding habits, and ball gowns were decided upon. Juliana was slightly overwhelmed by the volume of costumes Sophia felt was necessary. By the time they had chosen ribbons, jets and beads for adornment, and examined the laces for trims, she had already lost count of her purchases and her head was spinning.

Finally, Juliana objected that one more evening gown of blue velvet trimmed with a wide satin collar was unnecessary, but Madame Bretin clucked and brushed her protests aside. Then she buttoned Juliana back into her old brown merino, which suddenly seemed very drab. With a determined look on her face, Madame Bretin turned to Sophia.

"If you will but change places with your niece, we shall begin with you now, Mrs. Thatcher."

Sophia rose leisurely, carefully removing the pins from her hat and placed it in Madame's outstretched hands before stepping in front of the mirrors. She studied herself briefly and smiled, the dimple hovering beside her mouth. "Yes, madame, I believe it is time to start on me."

• • •

Exactly ten days later Madame Bretin's messengers delivered box upon box to Wentworth House. Claire, a trusted finisher, accompanied the order to make any last minute adjustments. Sophia and Juliana had Smithers bring two standing mirrors to the small reception room on the third floor and spent a delightful afternoon rediscovering their many purchases. They exclaimed with pleasure again and again after trying on all their new finery.

Claire was needed only for a loose button because Madame had achieved her reputation by precision work. Each confection was almost a work of art, fitted perfectly to the figure and crafted with exquisitely set, fine stitches. The *pièce de résistance*, though, was Juliana's turquoise silk ball gown. A delicate shade that complimented her eyes, deepening them to azure; it was a color that would stand out against the pastels and whites of the debutantes at Charlotte Grenville's come out. Juliana swept a deep curtsy and peeped up into the mirror to find her aunt watching in delight.

"This gown should find you a widower or two, my love."

"Why Aunt," she began in reproving tones, only to catch sight of her breasts straining against the low décolletage of the gown. In a more sober tone she continued, "This gown will attract every rake in London. Claire, we must raise the bodice."

"Oh, no! Madame Bretin would have my head!" Claire was adamant. "No! No! Do not touch it! The gown is most becoming as it is. Why all the great ladies cut their gowns like this. Some even more daringly."

"Leave be, Juliana, dear. We wouldn't want to cost Claire her position. You'll just have to be careful not to curtsy quite so deeply." Sophia waved her hand dismissively and Claire left quickly, relieved that Madame's creation would remain untouched.

On the night of Charlotte Grenville's ball, Smithers ushered Monsieur Henri out of Juliana's boudoir, but before he closed the doors he permitted himself the very faintest of smiles. "If

I may so, ma'am, both you and Mrs. Thatcher are in quite good looks this evening."

"Thank you," Juliana said softly, watching his reflection in her mirror. Sophia came and stood behind her, surveying the Frenchman's work. He had cut Juliana's thick, silky curls so that they were a riot of ringlets framing her heart-shaped face and causing her green eyes to look enormous. Twining turquoise ribbons in and out through the curls, Monsieur Henri had arranged her shorter hair into an elegant coiffure.

Now when she looked into the glass she did not see the Juliana Grenville who had left Wentworth Park such a short time ago, but the creation of London's finest modiste and hairdresser. This new Juliana had even been so bold, she had darkened her eyelashes. She found she rather liked the exotic creature staring back at her. Smiling, she caught her aunt's gaze.

Juliana had never seen Sophia look so beautiful. Monsieur Henri had trimmed her hair to shoulder length and then pulled it up into a cornet of curls with a few wisps falling softly about her face. To this he had added a gray ostrich plume that exactly matched her eyes and the ball gown of heavy satin that Madame Bretin had designed.

"Well, my dear, do you think we shall do?" questioned Sophia.

Juliana turned, the gown swirling provocatively around her legs, and circled her aunt. She noticed how her satin gown shimmered to life in the candlelight and how the color made Sophia's remarkable eyes seem to glitter. If she had changed since leaving Wentworth Park, then so had her aunt. There was a gaiety about Sophia now that softened the strong bones of her face and, with the new gowns, her fuller figure was shown to best advantage. She was a mature woman at the height of her beauty, and from the gleam in her eye Juliana suddenly realized she was planning to enjoy herself to the fullest.

"You look lovely!" she exclaimed. "I wouldn't be surprised if it is you who finds a husband."

Sophia laughed, grabbing Juliana's hand. "Then let us be off to see what this evening holds for us."

In the carriage, Juliana's mind was so occupied with her plan to humble the marquis that she barely noticed the crush of carriages lining the street in both directions in front of the Grenville town house. Her own elegant landau, with two postilions, a driver, and a groom moved slowly forward until at last they were positioned directly in front of the door. Only then would Sophia permit them to alight.

She had only a fleeting impression of the Grenville mansion: black marble pillars, a chessboard-patterned floor, and everywhere glittering crystal chandeliers, and colorful arrangements of fresh flowers, as Sophia bustled her into a side room to deposit her cloak. The *ton*, like Juliana and Sophia, had visited their hairdressers, modistes, milliners, and sent their jewels for cleaning, all in preparation for this, one of the first balls of the Season. Now dozens of fashionably dressed guests talked and moved about the house—it was a mad crush, the highest accolade for a *ton* party.

Ascending the staircase to the reception line was a slow task, and Juliana had plenty of time to take in the glamour around her. Much to her disgust she did not spy the marquis. But she was charmed by the number of people who remembered her aunt and greeted her warmly. When they finally reached the reception line, she was surprised to see Lady Grenville's fixed smile change abruptly into a mask of frosty disapproval.

"Sophia, I can't imagine how you would allow…"

Charlotte stepped forward, so discreetly, that no one, not even her mother, realized how she effectively squelched Lady Grenville's outburst.

"Juliana, you look beautiful! You'll put everyone in the shade tonight."

A pleasant warmth crept through her, for in all truth she was still uncertain of the bodice. "You look especially lovely tonight also," Juliana returned, lightly squeezing her friend's hand. "Your gown is exquisite."

The empire line of the simple white satin set off Charlotte's tall, willowy figure to advantage and quite took her out of comparison to the usual debutante frills.

Charlotte shrugged good-naturedly. "Well enough. But we all pale beside you."

"Charlotte! You mustn't turn Juliana's head with such outrageous flattery," Lady Grenville twittered, fanning herself briskly with a large fan of magenta feathers, which exactly matched her satin gown.

"I never flatter, Mama. It is only the truth, as you very well know," her daughter replied calmly before turning back to place a kiss on Sophia's cheek. "I was hoping George would be with you tonight."

"Sorry, dear." Sophia patted her arm. "There still seems to be a problem with that field of wheat. But he promises to arrive within a few days."

"He did quite right to stay at home," Charlotte nodded. "The wheat is much more important than my ball."

After a brief smile at Lady Grenville, who still, for some reason, positively glowered at her, Juliana moved away, trailed by Sophia.

"I think Charlotte truly believes the crops are more important than her ball," Sophia murmured in disbelief.

"Of course she believes it. Charlotte never says anything she doesn't mean," Juliana replied absently, scanning the ballroom once again. Drat the man! Where was he? She had gone to all this trouble to dazzle him and he didn't even have the good grace to be here to witness her arrival!

Who is the chit looking for so earnestly? Dominic stood in a sheltered alcove from where he had been following their progress up the stairs. He felt a pang of some strong emotion which, if he didn't know better, he might think was jealousy. Juliana looked ravishing, but what was Sophia thinking about to let her wear such a dress? He stepped forward, pulled toward her by the attraction that always seemed to flare up whenever he saw her. But then he stopped, remembering who she was. No point in continuing, she could never be his. Although, the fascination he felt for her couldn't be denied.

Whatever had she done to her hair? Was it still as sweet-scented as it had been tumbling over his arm as he carried her to the Blue Boar Inn? She was quite simply the most beautiful woman in the room. But she was more than just a lovely woman outwardly displaying her charms. He knew from Will's stories and his own dreams of her that her beauty came from within— her spirit, the warmth of her soul, the truth in her eyes reflected a beauty that no other woman at the ball could ever hope to attain. And although the town bronze became her, he remembered her even more beautiful than this—sitting in the Forbes's garden lost in the spell of gypsy music…

A sturdy elbow nudged him sharply in the side and Dominic stiffened.

"My boy, who is that ravishing redhead who has just entered? Never seen her before." Lord Rodney raised a large quizzing glass that hideously magnified one watery blue eye.

Dominic couldn't help but smile at his uncle's entranced expression. Rod was one of the few beings left on earth for whom Dominic felt affection. "Her name is Juliana Grenville. She's the widow of Sir Timothy Grenville's son, Will."

"Remember Sir Timothy. Quite a pleasant place in Berkshire I recall."

"Yes. The Willows. Belongs to Sir Alfred and Lady Grenville now."

"Damn pushy woman Lady Grenville. Can't imagine what your grandmother's thinking of, throwing the family's support into her chit's come out."

"Afraid I do," Dominic muttered, but his uncle wasn't paying any attention. He was raising his quizzing glass again, peering openmouthed at Sophia.

"The woman next to the redhead. Who is she?"

"Sophia Thatcher. Juliana's aunt."

"Thatcher … Thatcher … don't ring a bell. But Sophia … Sophia. I can't quite place her. I … I don't believe it! Sophia Vane! My god, it's Sophia Vane!" he sputtered.

Totally oblivious to the damage done to Dominic's exquisitely fitted coat, Rodney gripped his arm, propelling him across the ballroom floor. "Come, my boy, must pay my respects." An almost boyish grin flitted across Rodney's ruddy face. "Never told anyone this, Dominic, but Sophia Vane nearly caught me twenty years ago."

Juliana, waiting for the first set to begin, was standing by an open French window hoping to catch any breeze that might stir into the already stuffy ballroom. She glanced around and saw Dominic, accompanied by an immensely overweight gentleman, walking toward her. Materializing out of nowhere, Sophia appeared at her side.

Conscious of Dominic's eyes on her, she again wished she had not allowed Madame Bretin to cut the bodice of this gown so deep. Madame had insisted it must be done to expose to best advantage her jewelry. But since Juliana wore only diamond earrings, long falls of small flawless stones that her father had presented to her upon her marriage to Will, all the dress exposed was herself. She had ignored her normal modesty because her need to best the marquis was stronger, and she felt sure this dress would attract his attention. Now with him in front of her, all her resolution fled before the first real smile he had given her since the Blue Boar Inn.

The portly gentleman, however, didn't spare her a glance. He had eyes only for Sophia.

Sophia extended her hand and her delightful smile brought the dimple hovering beside her mouth. "Rodney, how good to see you again."

Lord Rodney raised her gloved fingers to his lips, and then kept them imprisoned between his palms. "Sophia, you haven't changed. You're still as beautiful as you were twenty years ago ... more so!"

Chuckling, Aunt Sophia raised her eyes to Juliana. "Rodney, I'd like you to meet my niece, Juliana Grenville."

He glanced briefly at her. "Charmed," he murmured vaguely before turning back to her aunt. "Why don't you go dance with Juliana, Dominic, so Sophia and I can have a nice, long chat."

"Heard that, you old dog!" interrupted Freddie's voice. "This is my dance with Juliana."

Shaking his head, a slow sensual smile moved across Dominic's marvelous face. "You heard my uncle, Freddie."

Taking Juliana's hand he placed it in the bend of his arm.

"It's robbery, Dominic!" Freddie good-naturedly called after them.

Her heart was pounding in her throat, but she managed to return over her shoulder as Dominic led her away, "The next two dances are yours, Freddie!"

The musicians hidden away in the gallery above them began at that moment the first strains of the first set—a waltz. Dominic drew her into his arms, holding her lightly. For an instant the intimacy of their embrace sent a tingling sensation through her and she stiffened. But she remembered her plan to best the marquis and decided she would treat him like George or Freddie or any other young man. Of course, he was not any other young man, he was Dominic, and he had kissed her in the garden. Pleasant but vague fantasies danced in her head as she forced herself to relax. They swept and swirled around the room, Juliana's feet barely touching the ground so expert was Dominic's lead.

Dominic was conscious of her slender, softly rounded body within his embrace and the sweet-smelling masses of auburn curls tickling his chin. There had been that in her eyes when she had first glanced up and seen him and it struck a cord within him just as it had in the garden of the Blue Boar.

Long ago there had been a young man inside Dominic who could have responded to Juliana and the feelings she evoked. There had still been a ghost of that young man in him when he had met Will Grenville on the Peninsula.

They had been of an age, he and Will. Their paths had crossed many times, for Dominic's spying activities for Wellington had kept him coming and going to camps the length and breadth of that battle-scarred piece of earth. Often at night he would sit over camp fires staring into the flames seeking answers to the questions that had driven him away from all he held dear. It was then that he had come to know Will, when men had talked of home. Dominic listened to tales of sweethearts, mothers, sisters, and wives. But Will Grenville had spun the most appealing of stories about his country estate and the child he had made his bride in the few weeks before he left for war. Will's stories of the young wife with the spirit of a lion and the heart of a lamb had in some small way touched the hard core that was becoming Dominic's soul. It was then that he had forged an image of her that he had tucked away, safe and clean, in his subconscious.

The years of corruption since those nights had been long, and the task of slowly destroying that part of himself that still cared about all that he had once held dear was nearly complete. The more unsavory his reputation became, the more every woman he wanted became his for the asking. And the one memory of his mother and his half brother that had scarred his soul burned brighter than ever.

But now he had met Juliana and come to know her. And to desire her in a way totally different than he had ever experienced. At the Blue Boar he had wanted nothing more than to cup her beautiful face in his hands and lower his mouth upon her softly yielding lips. And he realized he wanted that still. Of course, that would never happen again, now that he realized who she was. Perhaps, that was what had drawn him to her, he speculated. He had known, somehow, that here at last was the woman he always wanted. She had pushed all the horrible memories, the promises he'd made to stop the taint within himself far away. Vibrant and alive, she was more than the memory of the young girl who had embodied all he had once wished for himself; she was everything any man could hope for.

The shock he'd experienced realizing Juliana was Will Grenville's bride—the very woman he had dreamed of—had jolted him to reality. He had withdrawn back behind the walls he had so carefully erected around himself long ago. He wouldn't allow himself to think about what might have been. It was too late for such folly. He must not forget that Juliana could never be for him; one night, long ago, had robbed him of the future. The man he had become did not deserve any happiness. Any chances to forget the taint. It was his legacy. His and Jules.

Dominic's arms tightened almost painfully about her and Juliana looked up, nearly crying aloud at what she saw on his face. How could a notorious rake like the Marquis of Aubrey look so sad and lonely?

"Pardon me, Dominic. But the music has stopped you know," said a crisp strong voice behind the marquis.

Juliana gazed around in surprise to discover the ballroom had fallen silent and that most of the dancers had already left the floor.

Dominic dropped his hands, stepping back from her. A tall, slightly graying, solemnly dressed gentleman with a distinctive military bearing stood beside him.

"I beg both an introduction and the next dance with your charming partner," the stranger requested quietly.

Dominic seemed to hesitate for the space of a heartbeat before bowing over her hand.

"Juliana Grenville, may I present William Seymour, Lord Edgemont."

Her curtsy was as natural as breathing, but she was giving the gentleman in front of her little thought, for she was still dazed by what she had seen in Dominic's eyes.

"A pleasure." Presenting his arm in a stiff, decorous manner, Lord Edgemont smiled charmingly. "May I have the honor of leading you out for the next dance?"

Juliana wished she and Dominic could be back in the garden at the Blue Boar, alone. For a moment the wall he had erected between them had fallen. She would have liked to explore the strange vulnerable being visible only momentarily, but he was gone.

Hardening her resolve, she remembered her plan. This man was not vulnerable, just another rake who knew women's softness and played fast and loose with all of them, even herself.

"I would be delighted, sir," Juliana answered, forcing herself to smile at Edgemont. Before she accepted his arm, she couldn't resist another look up at Dominic, scanning the perfection of his features, seeking a glimpse of the man she had so briefly seen. He was gone.

"Thank you, my lord marquis." She steeled her voice. "I enjoyed our waltz."

For an instant she thought he would respond with nothing

but a cool nod, but instead she saw the Dominic who had walked with her in Mrs. Forbes's garden, as his wonderful smile transformed his face.

"I too, Juliana."

Why did he play this game with her? First he was one man and then another. She wanted to stay with him, to talk to him, to touch him again. But there was nothing to do except place her hand upon Lord Edgemont's sleeve and allow him to lead her away into the next set.

From the side of the ballroom Dominic watched as Edgemont led her through the patterns of the country dance.

"Didn't take him long." Dominic glanced around as Freddie's strolled up, a half-empty champagne glass held loosely in his fingers. "Heard he was on the lookout for a wife. The late Lady Edgemont left a brood of five children in Dorset they say."

"Shouldn't listen to idle gossip, Freddie," Dominic said absently watching Juliana grapevine, toe point, and cross to the music.

"Don't. Just thought I'd warn you on the chance you've changed your opinion of dashing young widows." Freddie searched Dominic's face carefully. "Watched your dancing. Never saw you hold anyone so correct and careful. Never saw you treat any woman with consideration for their reputation before. You had a certain look I've never seen before. Except with Juliana."

"I haven't changed, Freddie." Turning away from the dancers, he took the champagne glass, tossing the contents down his throat, and placed it back in Freddie's hand. "Ah ... the delectable Dora has just arrived. I mustn't keep her waiting."

Juliana glanced back to where she had last seen Dominic, but he was no longer there. Crossing to the next form, she turned to face her partner and over his shoulder she saw Dominic with Lady Dora Stanwood. The raven-haired beauty was laughing and nearly leaning against him, giving him every opportunity to view her indecently shallow bodice.

The look on Dominic's face was one of sensual pleasure. There was nothing of the vulnerable man who had so deeply touched her heart as they danced. Juliana missed a step, but quickly regained it and her senses. Lonely and sad … the Marquis of Aubrey! Obviously it had all been the trick of candlelight. He was indeed the heartless flirt Freddie had described to her, and it would give her great pleasure to put him firmly in his place!

After hours of pretending to Aunt Sophia, to Lord Rodney, who curiously enough remained firmly attached to her aunt's side, to Lord Edgemont, to Freddie, and to everyone else that she had never spent a happier evening in her life, Juliana had a raging headache. She watched without pleasure as Dora Stanwood demonstrated to the *ton* that Dominic was hers. He did not seem to be objecting. In fact, he was positively encouraging her advances. No doubt that was the way of notorious rakes.

Forcing herself to look away from where Dominic, his golden head bent, concentrated on something Dora was saying, she tried to focus on Edgemont, who had kindly produced a glass of lemon squash for her. He was the perfect man. A titled widower with children and a home to care for. Just what she had come to town to find. He certainly seemed smitten with her, dancing every dance allowed and taking her down to dinner. He was charming and handsome in a dignified, soldierly way. He had been speaking to her for the last few minutes and she had not the vaguest notion as to what they were discussing. Why didn't he just go away and leave her alone for a few minutes? Would this evening never end?

Late that night, mercifully alone at last, Juliana sat before her mirror in a light shift while she carefully pulled at the narrow turquoise ribbons still threaded through her curls.

Without knocking, Sophia opened the bedchamber door and entered, closing it behind her.

A small half smile curved her mouth as she came forward to the dressing table and sat on the small rosewood chair beside the mirror.

Juliana watched her out of the corner of her eye while continuing to tug at her ribbons. "You certainly look pleased with yourself. I must say I don't blame you. Lord Rodney is charming."

"Yes, he is, my dear. In fact, I have quite made up my mind to marry him this time."

Juliana dropped her hairbrush, and several crystal bottles adorning her dressing table rocked precariously and then tumbled over.

Sophia laughed. "The expression on your face, love, reminds me of young Ben's when Dominic gave him the gold coin for attending to his horses."

"Are you sure, Aunt Sophia?" Juliana leaned back in her chair.

"Of course, I'm sure. Rodney obviously needs me. If he doesn't call a halt soon, his corset won't even be able to contain him."

"Aunt Sophia!"

Her aunt nodded solemnly. "I heard it creak when he sat down. He tried to cover it with a cough but failed." Her lips became a firm line and there was a certain glow in her usually calm eyes, which Juliana knew from past experience did not bode well for Lord Rodney.

"Within six months of my care he will have no need of his corset. Then he will have some semblance of his old looks back. He was once nearly as devastating as Dominic. In fact, I fancied myself in love with Rodney until dear Cornelius arrived in town and literally swept me off my feet."

"Uncle Corny!" Juliana squelched a nearly overwhelming desire to laugh. Uncle Cornelius had looked less like a romantic hero than anyone she had ever seen. Just a bare inch or two taller than her aunt, he had had a slight physique, thin hair, and nearly colorless eyes. Juliana had loved him dearly, but she could hardly credit Aunt Sophia choosing him over someone as dazzling as Dominic.

Her aunt obviously saw the disbelief on her face. "I know it is difficult for you to understand, dear. But sometimes there is a certain attraction between two people that has nothing to do with their looks or their station."

"Remember, I've been in love and married myself," Juliana reminded her gently.

"For exactly eighteen days to a boy who was like a brother to you."

Juliana felt heat rise in her chest. Not only did she possess her father's red hair, but also his temper.

"I assure you that we did not live as brother and sister for the short time we were together! I have very special memories of our marriage," she replied in as angry a voice as she had ever used to her beloved aunt.

"Do you plan to live on those memories for the rest of your life? Because quite frankly they make for rather unsatisfactory bedfellows," Sophia said with a sternness that stung Juliana into replying even more sharply.

"I have said I would find a husband, haven't I?"

"Oh, yes ... your lonely widower." Aunt Sophia continued to observe her closely, her voice softening. "Edgemont, perhaps. But he would never replace Will, would he? You would do your duty, of course, but you would never give him any part of yourself that you gave Will."

Juliana wanted to look away from her aunt's knowing eyes, but her pride wouldn't allow it.

"No one can ever replace Will, Aunt Sophia. I promised his father I would never forget him. It is the least I can do since I failed them both by not producing an heir."

"If that is so, what do you intend to do about the Marquis of Aubrey?"

Juliana did look away then, straightening the crystal bottles and ribbons strewn across her dressing table.

"Dominic has nothing to do with it." She shrugged. "I cannot imagine why you ask."

"Can't you? I'm not blind. He affects you. I saw it at the inn and again here in London. But never so clearly as when you danced tonight. There was a moment when you both looked so ... vulnerable." Then Sophia had glimpsed it, too, that searing pain and loneliness on Dominic's face that made Juliana want to cradle him against her breasts to soothe away all the hurt. Lifting her chin, this time she did not flinch from her aunt's gaze.

"I am not vulnerable to the marquis. I will admit that I found him entertaining at the Blue Boar. And he was kind to us there, but obviously because he had nothing better to do. For you must agree that his behavior has changed since we arrived in London. In fact, I find his treatment despicable. Which only proves that he really is a conceited flirt and a rake. I refuse to let him get away with his shabby treatment of us. I plan to put him in his place!" Folding her hands in her lap, Sophia frowned. "You have surprised me, Juliana."

"I know it is an entirely unworthy goal I've set myself, but do not try to dissuade me, Aunt!"

"No, my dear, I would not think of trying. But my surprise stems from something quite different." Sophia rose, gathering her gown tightly around her. " I have seen you infatuated, as you were with Will from the time you were thirteen years old. I've seen you glowing with excitement the few weeks you spent together as man and wife. And I've seen you totally indifferent to suitor after suitor. But I have never, never seen you so passionate about anyone or anything as you are about Dominic." At the door Sophia turned back to her, her gray eyes wide and thoughtful. "I think, my darling, you should give serious thought to just where in your life Dominic's place is. And whether or not he has already a place in your heart."

Juliana sat stunned as the door closed behind her aunt until a fiery rage ignited within her. With a swipe of her arm she sent the hairbrush flying against the wall. "This time, Aunt Sophia, you are wrong! I won't forget Will! Not for Dominic! Not for anyone! I promised..."

Memories crowded into her mind: Will with his ebony curls and deep brown eyes, Will, whom she had loved. He had in his shy-boyish way stirred the only embers of passion she had ever known until now. It was a gentle warmth that memories of Will, his father, the Willows, and Wentworth Park brought. Only since she left Berkshire had she felt this restlessness, this yearning for something more.

Shaking her head, she peered at her reflection and lifted her left eyebrow while lowering her right, a trick which had always made Will and her family fall into fits of laughter. She needed to be reminded of those happy, carefree times. She smiled. "Just remember who you are, Juliana Vane Grenville. And what you set out to do. Place George firmly in the bosom of the *ton*. And find a nice comfortable widower so your brother can get on with his own life. Nothing has changed! Nothing!"

She opened her jewel box and took out the gold locket, carefully scanning Will's likeness. Yes, it was just as she recalled. For one sickening instant she had not been able to see him clearly in her mind. She must never allow that to happen, for she had given her word. Father had taught her well: the Vane word of honor was not given lightly.

Chapter 6

It was an unusually animated Rodney Crawford who hammered on the Vane town house door two days later. He was reluctantly joined by his amused nephew. A smile curled Dominic's mouth for he had never seen his uncle so excited. Not at a mill when his man was winning, not even at cards. Nothing that Dominic could remember had ever brought this particular look to his uncle's face.

The urgency of Rod's knocking did not cause the door to open with more than usual dispatch. The imperturbable Smithers opened it with no trace of having hurried.

"If you will wait in the small parlor, Mrs. Thatcher will receive you momentarily," Smithers said as he ushered them into the comfortable room Dominic had visited once before.

Dominic looked at the bountiful flower arrangements and lack of clutter that so clearly represented Juliana's hand; he was consumed with schooling his demeanor, determined that his carefully cultivated facade would not slip. Once again he was subjecting himself to sweet torment, like a moth battering itself against the window at twilight desperate to reach the candle flame that would consume it. He was many things, but not a coward. That was why he had agreed to the morning call with Freddie, and again today with Rod. His walls of defense were built high and strong, fortified over the years of passionless embrace with many women who had never touched him except physically. This one woman would not breach them and so he would prove to himself. There was enough honor left to him that he knew what he must do.

Sophia found Dominic leaning against the mantel dressed with careless elegance in a chocolate brown coat, whipcord breeches and tan leather boots; while Rodney, splendidly attired in correct morning clothes, reclined uneasily upon a narrow bench, which sagged a little with his weight. He rose with remarkable agility when she entered.

"Sophia…," Rodney breathed her name once as if it were a greeting, and reaching out, raised her fingers to his lips.

"Your servant, Sophia," Dominic said to her, a complacent smile hovering at the corners of his mouth.

Sophia sank down upon the settee and Rodney joined her, once again retaining her hand between his large palms. She sighed. "Please excuse my niece for not attending you, but we have an illness in the house."

"Juliana?" asked Dominic sharply, all trace of satisfied boredom suddenly gone. "Is she ill?"

Sophia hesitated, studying him for a moment. "No. Although she will be if she does not give over some of our nursing duties. It is young Ben, the postboy … perhaps you remember him from the day of the accident, Dominic?"

"Carrot-topped lad? Face full of freckles?"

"Yes. He is Benjamin's only son. His mother died last spring. Juliana is quite fond of him … as she is of all the children at the Park. Insisted on moving him down to the spare bedroom next to her own, and is nursing him herself. She has hardly slept since he fell ill."

Rodney stroked her hand, which Sophia found surprisingly soothing. "Has a physician been called?" he asked.

"Last evening. He calls back today. He said all the spots should be out by then. But the fever is still raging … I trust you have both had the measles?"

"Yes, in the nursery. You had them, too, Dominic. I remember you were one big spot."

A light smile played at the corners of Dominic's lips and he laughed. "I can't recall, Uncle."

"Take my word for it, my boy. Your mother cared for you with just such devotion as Juliana is giving young Ben."

Sophia saw it again, just as she had in the parlor of the Blue Boar Inn. One moment Dominic was leaning leisurely against the mantel, a self-assured smile on his appealing face, and the next instant there was something in his eyes and a tightness across his lips that she did not understand.

His beautifully shaped mouth curled into a sneer. "Hah! Motherly devotion from Leticia! Surely you jest, Uncle. She was much too busy with her lovers!"

Sophia's gaze was fixed on Dominic's face, and she felt the flush creep up her cheeks when she saw his cornflower blue eyes darken to almost navy in disgust. "The black widow did not nurse her children. She destroyed them," Dominic declared fiercely.

His words hung, echoing like distant thunder on a sultry summer night when the air is heavy and one can feel the power of a storm building all around. Sophia's face must have mirrored her horror at his words, for suddenly he was staring appalled into her startled eyes, and without a word of regret, he turned and walked quickly from the room, the door slamming shut behind him.

"Damn my fool tongue!" In a rough voice Rodney broke the spell.

Sophia looked at him, trying to gather her thoughts and make some sense of all Dominic had said, and all that had not been said, but that could be read in the shadows marring his face. "I do not understand, Rodney," she said softly.

"Of course, you do not, my dear. I hardly understand it myself!" His harsh voice betrayed the depths of his feelings, but seeing Sophia's shocked face his expression softened. "It was nothing you did. It was me. I should never have mentioned his mother. It was my mother that nursed him, of course. Leticia didn't come near the sickroom for fear she would be infected. Or Jules."

"Jules?"

"Dominic's older brother by five years." Frowning, Sophia shook her head. "Older brother? Then how is Dominic the marquis?"

"Leticia was a widow with a young son when Charles met her. She was French you know. Married the Comte de Saville when she was young. After his death she came here visiting relatives. Charles met her and married her within a month."

Sophia was silent. There was more here than Rodney was telling. Much more. "She and Charles were happy, I presume," she probed finally, searching for the right words. "I mean, of course, they were pleased to have such a handsome son as Dominic."

Shrugging, Rodney lowered his eyes. "Suppose so. Wasn't that close to my brother at the time, Oxford and then on the town you know."

She studied his downcast face for a moment before standing and moving to the empty fireplace, staring at it moodily for several minutes. Making her decision, she turned back to him. "I hope I do not speak too frankly when I say that since we have met again I feel that, this time, we may become even closer."

"It is my fondest hope," Rodney replied softly, for an instant looking nearly as young as he had twenty years ago.

Going back to the settee, Sophia sank down beside him. "Then I wish to know about Dominic and his mother. Am I being too forward, my dear?"

Grasping her hand, Rodney studied her long, thin fingers, his head bowed. "It is not my place to tell, Sophia, since I do not know it all."

"I have grown very fond of Dominic and would help if I could. Perhaps you could tell me what you do know," Sophia ventured.

"Yes. Of course." His voice firm, Rodney looked at her with great seriousness narrowing his pale blue eyes. "Leticia's beauty hid her true nature from all of us. If you had seen her, you would understand. She cajoled everyone with her radiant smile and black flashing eyes. She had that French vitality that sparkles and draws you to its flame ... But after she produced an heir, she locked her bedroom door against Charles."

Rodney stopped, but Sophia tightened her grasp on his fingers urging him on. "What a deplorable marriage in which to rear children! But what of Leticia's relationship with Dominic and Jules?"

"She had very little time for Dominic, although for some reason he adored her. She devoted all her time and energy to her own comforts and those of Jules. Dominic loved his brother. But I always felt he was hurt that Leticia seemed to love Jules more than him." Rodney shook his head, squeezing her hands a bit tighter. "Not Jules's fault. It was Leticia who was possessive of him, almost unnaturally so. She called him her 'little count.' Perhaps because he is the image of his late father. She would always compare Charles to Jules's father ... and her other lovers."

"Well," Sophia stated matter-of-factly, "It is not unknown in the *ton* for ladies to take lovers."

"Sophia, you don't understand! She flaunted her affairs in front of Charles. No one was safe from her. Even I..." Rodney looked away, his chubby cheeks crimson.

"Oh, no, Rod!" Sophia moved closer to him, placing her hand over their clenched fingers, trying desperately to keep the shock out of her voice.

She obviously failed, for Rodney's head shot up, his pale blue eyes wide. "Good God, Sophia, I didn't ... I mean .... there she was stark naked in my bed ... didn't know she was there ... ran all the way to the stables and fled to London. Had the devil's own time explaining my abrupt departure to the duke."

Sophia was surprised at the relief she felt at Rodney's confession and at the growing affection he inspired. But she would consider that later. Now she must concentrate on Dominic.

"If Dominic was devoted to his mother, when did he turn against her? When he grew older and saw what kind of person she was?"

"No ... it was not until after the accident that he saw her for what she had been."

Sophia's insides coiled with fear when she saw the look of pain and dread on Rodney's face, but she forced him on. "Tell me about the accident."

"Never been fully explained," he began, his voice sinking to a shadow of its former self. "Leticia was shot by my brother Charles in a drunken rage. Jules was wounded. No one knows how. Then ... then Charles ... Charles turned the pistol on himself. Dominic was there, but unable to stop it."

• • •

The day had barely edged into evening when Sophia quietly entered the blue bedchamber next to her niece's. A large four-poster dominated the panels of carved oak painted pale blue and white, and the delicate furnishings upholstered in striped silk placed about the room. Juliana sat on one fragile chair pulled close to the bed.

She was watching the gentle rhythm of Ben's breathing, his thin chest rising and falling beneath the fine blue cover. Lifting one of his hands that lay palm up, she cupped it against her cheek for a moment before carefully resting it back on the quilt.

Suddenly she looked around and Sophia could see the sheen of tears on her cheeks.

"The fever has broken," she whispered softly.

Sophia stood beside the bed watching Ben, his freckles and spots so intermingled it was difficult in the candlelight to tell where one began and the other ended. Nodding her head, she placed a large vase of lavender and pinks upon the nightstand. "He'll be fine now, my dear. But we will be nursing you if you do not eat something. Come with me now. Cook has prepared a light supper for us."

Juliana rang for her dresser, Maitland, to sit with young Ben, leaving careful instructions that she be called if the boy woke. Then she asked Smithers to send word to the stables that Ben was, at last, out of danger.

Sophia and Juliana entered the informal dining room set with two places, and steaming serving dishes already laid out along the oak sideboard so they could serve themselves just as Sophia had ordered. The warmth from a small fire mingled with the scent of roses.

Juliana sank into a chair stroking a rose petal with a long, thin finger. "More flowers, Aunt Sophia?"

Sophia placed a crest-embossed china plate piled with breast of chicken poached in cream, asparagus, and small carrots in front of her weary niece before going back for her own.

"Dominic sent several bouquets. There are violets in our

bedrooms and a gardenia basket in the front parlor. He also sent a basket of strawberries and a pail of fresh cream for our young patient."

A slight frown creased Juliana's brow. "How did Dominic know about Ben? Smithers was told to send away all visitors."

"Smithers is a law unto himself as you very well know. He admitted Rodney and Dominic this morning, and as I happened to be in the upstairs hall I spoke to them briefly. Obviously Dominic felt flowers and fruit would brighten the sickroom."

"Very generous," Juliana said thoughtfully. "He has a way of surprising one, doesn't he? One moment the dashing knight-errant rescuing us. The next a distant stranger, and now this kindness."

An aching tenderness swelled in Sophia's breast at the tired, wistful smile on Juliana's drawn face. She wanted so much for her to be happy! She had begun to think she had found Juliana's ideal man until this morning. "A way of surprising one?" Oh, yes, Dominic could do that, indeed! She did not tell her niece that with the dozens of flowers, the fruit and the cream, there had been a note. A bold sprawl in black ink saying simply, "Forgive me."

One week later, Sophia caught sight of the tail end of a nightshirt disappearing up the back staircase. "Ben, what are you doing out of your bedchamber!"

"It be for Miss Juliana," Ben replied quickly, coming back down the steps. "Scones and tea from Cook. See."

Sophia examined the neat tray that Cook had obviously prepared for him. "Juliana would never have sent you. Why didn't she ring for a maid?"

"Fell asleep whiles readin' me a story. Looks poorly she does. Thought't might make her feel better. Did it meself," he said proudly.

Sighing, Sophia admitted she was much too lax with the servants, but Ben's smiling face flushed with fading measles made her stroke his tousled hair. "That was very thoughtful. But you must stay in bed and get well. Then Miss Juliana will no longer look poorly. Go on now."

Hurrying from the back hallway, her mind occupied with Juliana, she nearly collided with Smithers.

"Madam, you have a visitor in the front parlor." Looking down his long nose at her, Sophia self-consciously straightened the bow of her cap.

"Thank you, Smithers." Deciding she really must take him in hand, she lifted her chin and gave him a frosty stare. "I trust our visitor has a name."

He sniffed. "It is teatime, so naturally your visitor is Lord Rodney Crawford."

Sophia found Rodney in the wing chair before the fireplace. He rose when she entered, raising her hand to his lips.

"Sophia, my dear, what is troubling you? Has the boy taken a turn for the worse?" he asked, leading her to the settee and settling in beside her.

"Rodney, you are so kind to be concerned. Ben is making fine progress. It is Juliana who worries me."

"Never say she's come down with measles!"

The look of distress on his chubby features brought a great rush of affection into Sophia's breast. Yes, Rodney would do just fine.

"No, no, it is not her health. It is my plan. How can it work if she never leaves the house?"

Confusion wrinkled his brow. "Don't quite see…"

"Rodney, dear, I tell you this in great confidence," she said gently and was rewarded with a worshipful smile. She leaned over the teapot and carefully added two spoonfuls of liquid from a small bottle to Rodney's teacup before handing it to him. "As you know Juliana was widowed six years ago and has remained at Wentworth Park caring for her brother. For some time I have been most concerned about her future. But until recently I could see no way through my dilemma. Then Juliana gave me my answer. She became concerned that George was not enjoying life so he should become part of the *ton*. Then she decided it was time she found a comfortable widower with children and let George get on with his life. That is when I hatched my plan."

Raising his quizzing glass, Rodney peered closely at her.

"Sophia, 'fraid I'm still a bit vague. What are we talking about?"

"Don't you see, Rodney. I conceived the plan to come to London to find her widower, thereby forcing George into the city and into the *ton*. But not for an instant did I intend for Juliana to settle for a stuffy widower with a brood of children. No! She must have someone like Dominic." Encountering his shocked stare, she patted his hand again. "Not Dominic precisely. Someone like Dominic. It is my fondest wish to see my sweet Juliana happily settled."

Lacing his fingers with hers, Rodney gazed at her solemnly. "If it is your wish, then it is also mine, Sophia dear."

There was a discreet knock at the door. Smithers entered, his usually impassive face twisted with disgust.

"Sorry to disturb you, madam. The housekeeper needs your assistance downstairs."

"Now, Smithers? Whatever is the problem?"

"Something about turning a parlor maid off without a character. Mrs. Nelson needs your approval." His rigid stance portrayed his dislike of airing staff problems in front of Lord Rodney.

Rodney cleared his throat. "Um, I believe I'll go now, Sophia." He rose and executed a portly bow. "Perhaps I'll be able to do something, um, about our previous conversation."

Sophia dimpled up at him. "I knew I could rely on you."

As Dominic turned onto the street, someone was walking away from Juliana's town house. Suddenly the man waved his walking stick and bellowed, "Dominic. Dominic Crawford!"

"Blast!" Dominic muttered under his breath, recognizing his Uncle Rodney waving at him frantically. After his childish outburst at Sophia, he had not intruded upon her with his presence, but it had become his habit to drive his high-perch phaeton past Wentworth House in the afternoon. It was unfortunate that today he had been caught.

"Dominic, what luck! Need a word with you, my boy."

With a nod from Dominic, his tiger jumped down to assist

Rodney onto the high seat. "How is Sophia? And the boy, Ben?" Dominic asked carefully.

"Fine. Fine. It is Juliana that…"

"Juliana!" His horses shied and he relaxed his tense grip on the reins as they trotted away. "She isn't ill?"

"No, no. Fine in that way. But Sophia is concerned that she ain't found a husband."

Dominic became aware of strange stirrings in his chest. "I wasn't aware Juliana was hanging out for a husband."

"She might not be keen on it. But Sophia's fondest wish is to find her a dashing husband. You for instance."

Permitting himself the smallest of smiles, Dominic glanced at his uncle. "I'm sure Sophia did not suggest me for this honor."

"Well, not precisely you. Someone like you. Must find a way to help Sophia. Do anything for the woman, Dominic. Dashed if I wouldn't … Just let me off here at White's."

Tossing the reins to his tiger, Dominic jumped down and assisted Rodney to the cobblestones. "Coming in are you, Dominic? Be thinking about likely candidates, will you, my boy? Mean a lot to me."

Leaving his uncle in the card room, Dominic opened the heavy doors to the library. The quietness of the room settled over him, and several of the older members glanced up from their deep wing chairs as he made his way to a desk. At a wave of his hand a servant brought paper, pen, and ink pot. He must do this quickly before he changed his mind. He knew how to help Sophia achieve her goal and this was the first step.

Quickly he penned a note and addressed it to Mrs. Juliana Grenville. Before he could change his mind, he gave it to the waiting servant with delivery instructions.

Sprawling back against the hard chair, he stared at nothing, letting himself remember those days at the inn when he had first realized Sophia was interested in eligible parties. He had found it amusing then. But that had been before he had discovered the only woman he had ever wanted and decided he could never have her. Now he would help find someone truly worthy of her. Someone as fine and decent as Will Grenville.

Three days later a scrawny maid in a lacy, bibless apron admitted Juliana to the front parlor where Sophia sat in front of a hot fire in the carved marble fireplace. The heat felt welcome to Juliana, for she could never seem to stay warm these days after her long, chilly vigil beside Ben's bed.

"Did you notice the family resemblance between our new parlor maid and Smithers?" Aunt Sophia remarked when she entered. "Bella is his first cousin twice removed. He promoted her from scullery maid."

Juliana laughed aloud for the first time in days because, with her rawboned hands and long chin, Bella did bear a striking resemblance to Julius, the one puppy her late papa had insisted on keeping from the last litter Claudius had sired. She knew Aunt Sophia had meant to make her relax and she had succeeded admirably.

This afternoon her aunt was clad in a jonquil frock with puffed sleeves that showed off her nicely rounded shoulders. With her dark hair pulled up in a yellow ribbon and small curls framing her face she looked younger than her thirty-nine years.

"Are you going out, Aunt Sophia?" Juliana asked, reclining on the settee.

"Yes. Rodney is taking me driving in the park just as he has every day this week," her aunt replied with a self-satisfied air, before turning a stern gray eye on her niece. "It certainly wouldn't hurt you to get some fresh air. Young Ben has been raising havoc in the kitchen for days. Even his father has ordered him back to his own quarters, but still you hover over him. The least you could do is accept Dominic's kind invitation to go for a short ride. You know you miss your horses dreadfully."

"Aunt Sophia."

"Don't tell me!" Aunt Sophia held up her hand to protest her niece's confidences. "What you do next to put poor Dominic in his place, I'd rather not know. He was goodness itself when Ben was sick. Sending fresh fruit every day and keeping the house full of flowers. But if you still harbor these absurd feelings of persecution, I want to hear none of them!" She sighed deeply, shaking her head. "Of course, you may be correct and I wrong. As your chaperon I should, perhaps, be encouraging you to stay away from such a rake."

Surprise widened Juliana's eyes. "Aunt Sophia, are you saying that Dominic is someone I should be protected from? If so, why do you wish me to ride with him?"

"Of course, you don't need to be protected from Dominic! Even though several ladies of the *ton* have made morning calls for the express purpose of informing me that Dominic is a rakehell. However, I, as you very well know, am an excellent judge of character." She waved her hand dismissively. "Believe me, my dear, if Dominic ever paid the slightest degree of attention to any one of their daughters, the tattle mongers would be in raptures, for he really is quite wonderful."

"You are right, Aunt Sophia, Dominic is ... has been wonderful since Ben's illness. I was foolish to say such things the night of the ball. Obviously I misjudged him. I will ride with him today."

Sophia gasped, nearly choking on a bonbon she had just popped into her mouth.

"Well, it is the least I can do," Juliana remarked, raising her chin in defense. "I have had both Freddie and Lord Edgemont to tea this week. It hardly seems fair to exclude Dominic when he has been so kind."

"Don't bristle at me, love. I couldn't agree more." Bella came in bearing tea, plain biscuits, and small plates of paper-thin sandwiches topped with watercress.

Juliana stared at the frugal fare. "Surely you aren't going to serve Lord Rodney this!"

"Of course. You have probably not noticed, but Rodney has already dropped over half a stone. Is that not marvelous? I hope he can continue to make such excellent progress without his elixir. It is nearly all gone."

"You have been giving his lordship Mrs. Forbes's potion!"

"Of course. I told you it might come in handy one day and so it has." Deciding the tea had steeped long enough, Aunt

Sophia took off the cozy and poured the steaming liquid into white teacups. "Drink your tea, dear, and then change for your outing. Wear that russet velvet habit. It looks magnificent with your coloring."

Juliana was ready thirty minutes before Dominic arrived. She watched for him from her bedroom windows. She paused only briefly in front of her mirror to arrange the short-crowned hat more becomingly over her curls and smooth out the skirt of the matching habit before she went to the head of the staircase.

When Smithers admitted the marquis into the foyer, a slight rustle of her skirt caught his attention. He glanced up and saw her. She seemed to glow when the sunlight filtering through the high windows caught her, making her velvet habit gleam and shine with her every movement as she descended the staircase. He resisted an impulse to go to her and catch her in his arms. Instead he waited for her to cross the foyer and then raised her gloved hand quickly to his lips.

"I'm pleased to see you, Juliana. You look lovely today," the trite conventional pleasantries he had mouthed to dozens of other women came easily to his lips.

Her smile was warm and sweet, as she had seldom given him, and he almost forgot his intentions. Almost. Rod had told him Sophia's fondest hope was to see her niece happily settled. That was why he had to proceed very carefully if he was to help Sophia attain her goal. And what little honor remained to him demanded that he help Sophia in her quest for Juliana's happiness. To be seen with the Marquis of Aubrey would bring Juliana's credit high, indeed: as long as he was very careful that his attention was not too marked. Too much attention and she would be fuel for the gossip mill just as he was. He knew his world well, and had carefully considered how to promote Juliana's interests. Somewhere in the *ton* there must be a man worthy of her, all she needed was to be brought to his notice. Freddie or Lord Edgemont, who seemed to be running tame in the house, were not quite fine enough, he had decided grimly.

Freddie had said Dominic's horses were among the finest in London, and he had not exaggerated. Dominic rode his white

Arabian stallion, Bucephalus. But for Juliana he had chosen a rich brown gelding with a proud carriage. She stroked its nose once before Dominic tossed her in the saddle.

"His name is Caesar and he is still fresh this morning," Dominic warned.

Juliana hid a small smile while they rode through the streets to Hyde Park. Dominic could have no way of knowing that she had often risen at dawn to ride bareback and shoeless through the fields of Berkshire before her marriage to Will.

A curricle raced past, far too close to her gelding, and she steadied the frightened animal quickly, leaning over and whispering into his neck. She straightened when she felt the horse relax back into a brisk walk.

"That was well-done, Juliana." Dominic gave her a breathtaking smile, which reached into his eyes deepening their color, drowning her in their depths. "You ride just as I knew you would."

His words and his smile made her dizzy with joy. Her heart pounded like a drum and her stomach knotted into a tight bow. It was not right for her to feel this way about this man. She knew it was wrong, terribly wrong. Dominic appeared to be many things to many different people. But to Juliana Vane Grenville he must be only a man who, for reasons she did not understand, extended kindnesses to her, which she accepted gratefully. To her he must be a friend, nothing more.

They passed through the stone posts at the park's entrance and turned down a bridle path that was still sparsely occupied. It was a bit early yet for the *ton*'s daily promenade. Dominic remained silent, and Juliana was grateful for the moments to relax and steady the uneven beat of her pulse. Her eyes roamed slowly over the park's rolling green hills, tall copse of trees, and wide fountains, whose sprays of water sparkled like diamond chips in the sunlight. Across the gardens the scent of hundreds of flowers perfumed the air.

Her lips parted in a smile. "It really is quite lovely you know."

He glanced around, an amused expression softening his face. "Is it? I must confess I haven't taken note of it for years."

He looked at her, almost grimly, she thought. "You have a way of making me see things in a new light."

The horses stopped, conspiring with the beauty of the park and the depth of sincerity in his voice to allow her to search his eyes.

He's sincere, she thought. If only he would stay this way: gentle and tender. If only I could understand his moods.

When a rider approached, Juliana looked away suddenly, confused by the intangible connection she felt to the marquis, as if they had been communing without words.

Lord Edgemont checked his horse and embraced her in such a warm smile that Juliana felt sure she blushed. "You ride like a goddess, Juliana," he effused, extending his hand to take her fingers. Peeling back her glove, he kissed her wrist lightly.

Embarrassment warred with a flash of triumph that Dominic should see that, at least in one quarter, she was a complete success. She quickly glanced up at him to gauge his reaction, but he appeared completely absorbed in flicking a speak of dust from his perfectly proportioned shoulder.

"Thank you, Lord Edgemont. You are very kind." She laughed lightly, a little higher pitched than usual, a habit when she was nervous. His lordship's rather intense pursuit, for she could think it nothing else when he had called every day this past week, was a bit unnerving. She was vastly relieved when Dominic gave him a cool nod and moved ahead so abruptly, with her gelding following, that Edgemont was forced to back up several paces and be left behind.

When Dominic finally slowed, she raised her eyebrows while he coolly inquired if she had wished to dally longer and perhaps have Edgemont join them.

"No." Juliana drew her horse alongside his. "I am very much enjoying myself with just the two of us."

"Good." The warmth she had felt and responded to in the Blue Boar Inn was back for an instant caressing her. "Edgemont is right. You ride like Diana. I believe you might even be able to handle Bucephalus."

Juliana was sure she went scarlet with pleasure. Such a

compliment from an acclaimed rider like the Marquis of Aubrey was praise, indeed. And she admitted ruefully, any compliment from Dominic was precious. "Thank you, my lord. I do not believe I have ever been compared to a goddess twice in one day!"

Juliana's light green eyes shone so brightly and her luscious cherry lips were curved in such a delicious smile that Dominic reached out to touch her flushed cheek, but a shrill female voice called his name, stilling his hand.

An open town carriage lacquered in red was stopped, blocking the path in both directions. Dominic and Juliana trotted carefully over to pay their respects to Lady Grenville and Charlotte.

As Dominic bent over her ladyship's hand, awkwardly extended over the carriage side, Juliana exchanged a fond smile of welcome with Charlotte.

"Dominic, my boy, how wonderful to see you! I received your note this morning. I can't tell you how happy it made me." Lady Grenville's full face actually seemed to glow with pleasure, reflecting the carriage upholstery—red with gold frogging. It matched her unfortunate choice of dress.

"Juliana, we haven't heard from you and Sophia as yet. Do you join us?" Charlotte asked eagerly.

Juliana looked puzzled. "I am sorry, but I do not understand."

Charlotte shot her mother a cool look before smiling up at her friend. "Your note must have gotten misplaced. We give a supper party at Vauxhall tomorrow evening. The marquis and Lord Rodney are joining us. I hope you and Sophia are free. Don't we, Mama?"

"Of course, of course," murmured Lady Grenville, merely favoring Juliana with a flick of her small, bulgy eyes. "I shall send another note around immediately."

"Thank you, Lady Grenville. We shall look forward to it," Juliana said quietly, a slight color rising in her cheeks.

Dominic again had an absurd wish to reach out and touch her. Damn Lady Grenville! The old biddy had never sent the note and Juliana knew it.

"We must take our leave. The horses grow restless," he said lazily moving away with a nod. He sensed that Juliana was eager to go on, and he had certainly had enough of Lady Grenville's company, although she had given him another opportunity to further Sophia's ambitions. Vauxhall with Juliana would fit nicely, all the young bloods would be there. By the end of the week she would be besieged with callers eager to follow in Aubrey's footsteps. He had seen it happen time and time again. He refused to acknowledge that this thought did not give him the pleasure it should.

He looked at her profile, strength evident in the high cheekbones and fine brow, vulnerability peeping through in her rapidly fluttering eyelashes and slightly pouted mouth. "Charlotte Grenville seems to be quite an intrepid girl for one so young," he offered blandly. Juliana relaxed her tight grip on the reins and her horse stopped fidgeting. She cast him a glance to see if he was mocking her, but he continued in the same bland tone, "With a Mama like that she must find a need for social facility."

Juliana smiled in response and he laughed, absurdly pleased that he had been able to bring that curve of delight to her beautiful mouth. "Follow me to the canter."

They took a side path, now little used, where they could let the horses go. Juliana was warned by only a side glance before he called, "Race me!" and their canter developed into a full-blown gallop. They were flouting convention by racing, but there was no one to witness their rackety behavior.

Juliana laughed, her hair tumbling from under her hat and her riding skirt billowing like a russet sail about her legs. Dominic's horse seemed to tire and she surged ahead, tasting victory, but in an instant he shot past to win.

Her heart pounded in her ears and her breath was deep, straining her breasts tightly against her well-fitted jacket. Confusion washed over her when she reached Dominic's side and felt his eyes touch her body and rise slowly to her face.

"Your hair looks magnificent falling about your shoulders, my dear, but it might be in our best interest if you were to pin it back up." His voice was low and sweetened with amusement.

He reached over and took the reins from her numb fingers. Bucephalus snorted once, blowing gently at the gelding as the two horses nosed each other familiarly. Juliana raised her hands, twisted the fallen coils of hair up, and pushed them under the brim of her hat. The ride had cleared away the cobwebs of confusion and hurt that Lady Grenville had spun. Everything seemed clearer and brighter and easier to understand. Everything except the man before her.

Dominic's gaze stilled her nervous hands and she lowered them slowly to her lap, her eyes searching his face seeking understanding. Slowly, a quiet contentment, a certainty of feeling filled her. Just like in the Blue Boar Inn garden, she could feel him reach out to her. Then he took one coil of hair, which still brushed her cheek, and curled it around his fingers.

"Your hair is like silk." She could not breathe while his fingers played inside the curl, his mouth curving slowly at the corners. "I always knew it would feel like this."

"Dominic, I…," she stumbled, hardly recognizing the hoarse whisper as her own voice.

Slowly, he unwound the curl from his fingers and let the tips of them lightly trace the curve of her chin. "We should go back now, Juliana."

She drew a deep, shuddering breath to control her disappointment as once again he shut the door between them. She would never comprehend this man. Just when she felt a breakthrough was imminent, he would withdraw. But this time, she strengthened her resolve. She would find a way to understand him. She had to try, for then she might understand this bond she felt between them.

He relinquished her reins and turned back toward the main thoroughfare.

"Thank you, my lord," Juliana's voice strengthened. "A canter was just what I needed."

He turned to her with his practiced smile, but instantly his pure cornflower eyes were unreadable, and she was surprised to see his hands tighten and pull Bucephalus to a standstill. Caesar moved several steps forward before she pulled him up to cast a nervous glance over her shoulder.

Dominic sat perfectly still, the sunlight spinning a soft halo around his hair and etching clear shadows about his set lips, a haunted look draining all the life from his face.

What have I done now, Juliana wondered, and looked blindly around. All that was visible was a lone horseman. He would have stood out even on the crowded thoroughfare, though, for he was dressed completely in black, relieved only by a snowy cravat and long ruffles at his wrists. She felt curiously uneasy at his approach. Then she noticed the dark riband and eye patch that dominated the left side of his face. His mount drew nearer and passed her as if she were invisible.

The dark man stopped inches away from Dominic and stilled his horse, leaning slightly forward in his saddle. "Ah, The Marquis of Aubrey." His right eyebrow lifted awaiting a response.

"What are you doing here, Jules?" Dominic asked in low, terse tones.

The dark horse shied, sensing the tension that swelled around them like gathering thunderclouds. Juliana controlled her own mount, which pranced uneasily in place, and held her breath, anticipating some monstrous action between the two adversaries. Old enemies, she judged, maybe the war.

"I've been to the Towers to visit their graces. Your grandparents were very welcoming."

"I told you I never wanted you on my lands again!"

"Ah, but Dominic," the sneer became more pronounced, "they are not your lands, yet. And the duke was delighted to see me." He narrowed his eye and spoke very distinctly. "The old boy invited me to make the Towers my home for as long as I want."

High-strung horses, held carefully in check, circled nervously, assessing each other as warily as the two men that sat them. Jules, in black, exuding practiced charm that couldn't quite cover a menacing tone. Dominic, in buff and tan, dropping all pretense of conventional manners to threaten quite openly.

Juliana's nerves tightened her hands. She prepared to thrust Caesar between the two, anything to break the ominous spell these men wove around each other. She knew she was completely forgotten as each stared unblinkingly into the other's face.

"Stay away from the Towers, Jules. And stay away from my grandparents. That is my final word." Dominic issued his challenge and Jules laughed softly. "We had an agreement. I expect you to abide by it!"

"Dominic, Dominic," Jules shook his head disbelievingly. "That was so long ago. And we were so young. Circumstances have changed."

Bucephalus surged forward and Dominic grabbed Jules's reins, forcing his horse's head around. "Nothing has changed!" Dominic bit out. "The agreement stands. Go back to France or wherever you've been."

Jules reached out, plucking the reins from Dominic's control, sidestepping his horse away from Bucephalus, and suddenly stopped, focusing upon Juliana for the first time.

"Charming. Utterly charming." He drawled, then turned to Dominic as if expecting an introduction. When none was forthcoming, he smiled mockingly. "My brother has forgotten his manners, my dear. I am Jules Devereaux, the Comte de Saville."

Juliana sat her horse in shock. Dominic had a brother! How could this be? "Juliana Grenville, monsieur." She replied as manners demanded. What was going on now was no joyous reunion between brothers, but something quite different. Whatever it was between these two men made her shiver in fear for them.

Jules maneuvered his horse close enough to take her hand. He lifted it to his mouth for a polite kiss, but Dominic forced his horse between them, separating them.

"Don't touch her!" His face was like frozen granite. "Come, Juliana. It is time I returned you to your aunt."

He whirled Bucephalus and, giving her no time for good-byes, urged their horses into a trot. Laughter echoed behind them.

"Dominic," instinct urged her to speak. "I did not know you had a brother."

"Half brother. His mother was a widow when she married my father. The only blood we share is hers."

Chapter 7

Vauxhall was gaiety itself! The colored lanterns strung in the trees, supper boxes discreetly hidden in leafy bowers, and strolling musicians all contributed to the relaxation of society's stringent rules. No wonder the *ton* adored an evening here!

Lady Grenville's party was seated at a choice table, close in enough for excellent service yet allowing privacy. Still, there had been a growing disharmony throughout the evening. Eugenia had seated Charlotte between Jules and Dominic and, although adroit in the delicate handling of her mother's faux pas, she definitely was not enough of a buffer for the two men. Juliana watched from across the table, seated protectively, and deliberately away from the eligible men, between Lord Rodney and Lord Grenville.

When the divertissement began after supper, Juliana was surprised that no one else seemed to notice how the air crackled between the two brothers. Although all could see that Dominic seethed with tension, apparently she alone recognized the strain Jules was under, for he appeared every bit the bored aristocrat, twirling his quizzing glass through his fingers. But though Jules seemed as absorbed in the port bottle as the other gentlemen of the party, Juliana had the oddest sensation that he was studying her.

Lady Eugenia's domination of the conversation was so complete that the rest of the party had fallen into a nearly stupefied silence. So the disquieting feeling grew with no one able to divert the company toward a more pleasant outlook. It was foolish to slip away from the box during one of the intervals, but Juliana had to get away from Jules's intense regard. And away from Dominic. He seemed so different tonight, not at all the pleasant companion of their ride in Hyde Park. Jules's arrival as escort to Charlotte and her mother had seen to that.

Her foolish plan to ensnare Dominic in spite, and teach him a long overdue lesson in humility, had been forgotten in the face of his kindness and consideration during Ben's illness.

She only wished she understood him better, for certainly they would soon be related. Lord Rodney had barely touched his supper tonight, and to a man who so obviously enjoyed his food, that could only mean he was in love or ailing. No one watching him gaze at Sophia would have any doubt as to the cause.

Mingling in the noisy crowd, Juliana eagerly drank in the unfamiliar sights and sounds of Vauxhall. She chose the Grand Cross Walk, which traversed the whole garden and turned onto the South Walk, to more closely examine the triumphal arches. Heady with the freedom she thought she had left behind in Berkshire, she wandered too far. Finally she realized she was quite alone. No other patrons had ventured beyond the last lighted arch. She rapidly retraced her steps, relieved not to encounter any stragglers. But her luck ran out; a group of boisterous young men, who had obviously been dipping at the bottle, blocked the walkway. Quickly ducking down a smaller, less lighted path, she thought to avoid them by circling back to the Grenville box. She knew that being alone at night was unthinkable for a lady of quality and at Vauxhall it was an invitation practiced by the fashionable impures. She could find herself in quite a fix.

Studying the many dimly lit pathways that wove their way through the darkness, she finally decided on a way that should, according to her sense of direction, bring her back to the well-lit and crowded thoroughfare.

This path was narrower, and overhanging branches made it seem very dark. Low bushes caught at her gown, and she had to stop once to untangle a vine that had somehow wrapped itself about her ankle. A few minutes more of wandering this thickly overgrown and dimly lit path forced her to admit she had made a dreadful error. She was not going in the right direction at all. The music was becoming fainter and the lamps were so far apart; she was more often in darkness than in their pools of light.

She stopped, trying to still her ragged breathing, and heard a rustle as if someone was hurriedly pushing aside the closely growing bushes behind her. Forcing herself to turn and look, she bit her lip, stopping a cry of fear, for a large shadow moved through the greater darkness.

Twirling around, she quickened her steps, moving deeper and deeper into the gardens. Heat warmed her cheeks and her breasts pushed against the bodice of her gown, for her breath came in deep painful gasps. Fear of what could so easily occur if she met a man in this dark, out-of-the-way place spurred her on.

Suddenly in front of her, out of the darkness, loomed a ruined temple. Rescue! Slipping inside, she looked around for somewhere to hide herself, but all the ruin contained was a stone bench and piles of dead leaves scattered about the floor. The stone wall seeped cold into her heated flesh as she pressed herself up against it and held her breath. Had she been quick enough? Had her pursuer seen her enter? Even as these thoughts came to her, a tall figure stepped into the moonlit doorway. Juliana's heart plummeted and for the first time in her life, she knew real terror.

Carefully, she backed several steps before turning to edge deeper into the shadows. She closed her eyes, momentarily relying on her childhood belief that if she couldn't see, she couldn't be seen. A pair of strong male arms grasped her waist and she screamed, struggling and kicking desperately at her assailant.

"Juliana, you're all right now!"

Incredibly through her haze of fear she heard the vibrant voice of the Marquis of Aubrey. Finally realizing that the arms that held her were Dominic's, she sobbed with relief and twisted around to fall into his embrace.

"Oh, Dominic, I was so frightened. I thought…" Unable to say the words, her voice broke. "I don't know what I thought."

Dominic pulled her close, holding her lightly in the haven of his arms. The hammering of her heart began to quiet, but not to its normal pace. And as the fear subsided a more potent emotion filled its place.

Her cheek rested against the soft ruffles of his evening shirt and her hands were curled in fists near his shoulders. Relaxing her fingers until her palms were flat against the warm brocade of his jacket, she pushed herself slowly back until she could look into his eyes. She felt a tensing of his arms across her back.

The air thinned when she took it into her lungs, making her suddenly breathless. Her body felt weightless where it rested along the length of his; weightless yet tingling with sensations. The caress of his jacket beneath her hands, the softness of his shirt pressing her breasts, the hard length of his thighs against hers: there in the dark she experienced touch in a way she had never done before. No, that was not true, she had felt this way once before: in Mrs. Forbes's garden filled with the echo of Romany music. It was like music: this feeling racing through her blood. She had longed to feel this again—with Dominic.

She remained absolutely still when Dominic raised his hands lightly onto her shoulders. "Don't be frightened, Juliana." It was the voice he had used in the garden, full of longing and desire. "Beautiful Juliana."

Coaxing her closer into his embrace with light urgings of his hands, his lips touched her forehead, her eyelids, the curve of her cheek, leaving a scorching trail on her moist, warm skin before, at last, he brought his mouth down upon hers. Cool and dry, he brushed his lips back and forth slowly until with a moan he covered her open mouth. Out of the darkness and the fear such an aching need filled her that she sobbed aloud.

They melded together. Each finely muscular inch of his body imprinted against her softness, and she felt how much he desired her. Strangely it did not frighten her, instead she felt exhilaration that he should want her so.

Their lips met again in a clinging kiss, deep and passionate, and she was embracing him tightly, as if she couldn't get close enough.

Whispering her name, his face buried at the side of her neck where her curls lay tangled, his deft fingers loosened the straps of her gown until her breasts were half exposed in the dim light. A thrill shook her as his mouth followed.

"You're so perfect," he breathed against her softness.

It was as if in this time and place there were no rules, no promises made, but only the discovery and joy that with this man she could feel as she had never felt before. She wanted it to go on and on.

The crackling of dead leaves crushed under foot, warned her an instant before a man coughed. "Ah, here you are, Juliana. Lady Grenville noticed your absence and sent me to find you."

Juliana tore herself out of Dominic's arms and spun around to find Jules lounging against the stone entrance to the temple.

Dominic caught her wrist in a painful grip and pushed her behind him. From somewhere, Juliana's senses returned, consuming her with shame.

The faint moonlight filtering into the ruin cast a pale aura about each man, causing Dominic's eyes to sparkle like sapphires and Jule's to glow with dark embers. The waves of anger from these two brothers pierced through her own deluge of shame and confusion.

"Don't make this more of a farce than it already is, Jules." Dominic's ragged voice was cold and flat, removing the last vestige of softness around Juliana's heart. "What is this game you are playing?"

Jules shrugged, his thin lips curving. "It is not I who am playing ... games, dear brother. I have simply come to chaperon the lovely Juliana back to the box before you are both in the suds."

His words stung her, but Juliana drew herself up with pride and stepped around Dominic to confront his brother.

"Thank you, Comte. It was foolish of me to slip away from the supper box for a stroll. I am only relieved it was you and the marquis who rescued me," she continued, determined to diffuse the embarrassing moment. Now, if Jules would only cooperate.

Laughing softly, Jules reached out and placed her hand on his arm. "It is my pleasure. Now, we return to the box and inform the others that Dominic took you on a short tour of the gardens. A bit rude not to include Charlotte, but he'll be forgiven. I will say I found you and joined in the stroll. Do you agree, Dominic?"

Relieved, Juliana tilted her head to gaze back at Dominic. He had remained perfectly still, his hands in tight fists at his side. He did not look at her, instead his eyes concentrated on his brother. To her dismay his face became the one of her nightmares.

"Mon frère, this time you are right," he mocked quietly.

Lady Grenville's fan snapped shut. Sophia and Rodney, lost in a private conversation of eyes, had stopped paying attention to her monologue some twenty minutes before when Jules had excused himself to greet acquaintances. Charlotte, forced to listen to her mother's diatribe against Juliana, had retreated to that private place in her mind she reserved for just these occasions.

"Charlotte, let this be a lesson to you." Lady Grenville's fan tapped the table, punctuating every word. "I knew we shouldn't have invited that woman. She's always doing something to draw attention to herself. Now it appears both Dominic and Jules have gone after her, and you are left here without an escort."

Without waiting for an answer, she swung around to a figure sitting well back in the shadows of the box. "Well, Sir Alfred? What have you to say to this?"

Whatever reply might have issued from this corner was effectively cut off by Charlotte.

"Mama. Here they are now. And Juliana … seems fine."

Lady Grenville's eyes narrowed with displeasure when Juliana approached. Jules had her hand tucked carefully in the crook of his arm and was animatedly describing the pigeons in Venice's St. Mark's Square. Very little of Juliana's composure had returned, but she was struggling to appear as natural as possible. Dominic, as always contemptuous of appearances, paced beside them, anger evident in every muscle.

"Ah, Lady Grenville. Such a lovely outing. Juliana has been delighting me with her observations on the crowd."

"Where have you…"

"Mama," Charlotte hurriedly broke in. "Perhaps the Comte and Dominic would like a port after their long walk. Could you get a waiter?"

Juliana sank into her chair between Lord Rodney and the empty space where Sir Alfred should have been, grateful to Charlotte for stepping in so adroitly. She knew Charlotte had not been deceived for a moment and was giving her an instant to recover herself before the full onslaught of Lady Grenville's questions would begin.

The port arrived and Lord Rodney roused himself to pronounce it very tolerable.

"Don't toss it down that way, my boy," he addressed Dominic. "Port should be rolled over the tongue, to savor it."

"Just so, my dear," approved Aunt Sophia. She turned to Juliana. "Did you have a pleasant stroll?"

The safest answer was to stay close to the truth Juliana thought. "Unfortunately, I wandered off on a side path and became confused."

"Hmph! I knew it," crowed Lady Grenville. "Sophia, you are a lamentable chaperon!"

"But it was quite alright, Lady Grenville," Juliana added quickly. "Dominic and Jules came and found me before I was quite lost." She looked at Jules and smiled at his bland expression. Although she tried not to, she couldn't keep her gaze from Dominic's face and then wished she could find the strength to look away, for not even in her worst dreams had his face been this hard mask.

Hours later, within the safety of her bedchamber at last, Juliana dropped to her knees beside her bed, laying her cheek against the smooth coolness of the satin spread. Exhausted from the strain of pretending that nothing had changed, when in reality her life had changed forever, she closed her eyes, forcing her mind to go back ... back to the past. To Will.

A terrible sadness swelled painfully in her chest. Will ... his boyish face ... the unruly halo of ebony curls ... That last day before he left for the Peninsula he had been so happy. So carefree. He rode away from the Willows eagerly, as if off to a parade.

She had tried to bear bravely the months of worry and loneliness, busying herself between responsibility at the Willows and at Wentworth Park, for their lands marched together. Her only pleasure, her weakness, was to ride beside the stream which divided their land, for it brought back such sweet memories of Will.

Will ... who she would never see again. She'd never forget the look on his father's face when the formal letter from the War Office was delivered by a young officer. Nor ever forget the torment that burned within her when she finally realized Will, who had been part of her life forever, was gone, forever.

She had tried to ease Sir Timothy's grief but had failed, being a constant reminder that she had not conceived during the brief marriage. Only once did he remark, "if there was to be a child, we would still have Will," but she saw it in his eyes every time he looked at her. The hurt and guilt nearly drove her to return to her home. But then Sir Timothy fell ill, and there was nothing she could do but stay beside his bed, grasping his hand as he talked of his son. Day after day until the last day, when finally, he had asked for her promise to remain faithful to Will's love and she had given it.

She opened her eyes, tears flowing down her cheeks, and looked at the locket laying in the palm of her hand. She opened it. Sir Timothy had bequeathed his dark eyes and unruly curls to his son. But there was a sweetness to Will's smile that his father had never possessed.

"I will never forget you, Will. You will always have a place in my heart." Sobbing, she wiped her wet cheeks with a corner of her gown. "I'm horrible ... horrible! I allowed him to kiss me ... touch me ... dear God ... I wanted him! Forgive me, Will ... please!" Shaking, she flung herself upon the bed twisting the bedcovers in her knotted fists while she wept. She cried for Will, who had been too young to die, for Sir Timothy, whom she had disappointed, and for herself.

It was a very long time before she could stop sobbing. She had dropped off to sleep for a short while, but had awakened again to her own muffled cries. At last her tears did stop, and she had to face the realization that she had broken her promise to Sir Timothy. Her plan for a safe future with a man who would never touch her heart, never have the power to hurt her again was shattered. She could never give herself to such a man, for the unthinkable had happened.

She had thought she would never love again, and surely this was as different from her feelings for Will as night from day; but it was love.

Pushing back the crumpled covers, she rose from the bed and went to the window to watch the first faint pink light beginning the new day. She was in love with the Marquis of Aubrey. In love with the greatest rake in the *ton*. A shameless flirt! And she loved him! He confused her, had hurt her, but he wanted her. She had seen it at the inn. And last night, would she ever be able to forget last night? She had wanted him, too. She had never felt so alive. Her body trembled now just remembering.

Moving away from the windows she went to the dressing table. Pulling open a drawer, she lifted out her jewel case.

"Good-bye, sweet Will. I shall never forget you. But it is time to put away the past."

Straightening her shoulders, she resolutely placed the locket in the ease and slowly closed the top.

Jules had nearly given up his search for Dominic when he made one last visit to White's near dawn and found him, in the library of all places, sprawled in a wing chair, a cup of coffee cooling between his palms.

Jules seated himself across the table and waited until Dominic lifted his heavy eyelids and sneered at him.

"Go away, Jules."

Flicking an invisible speck of lint from his trousers, Jules surveyed his younger brother. "Why are you carrying on so? All you did was steal a kiss from the chit in the moonlight," he drawled.

That must have struck a nerve for Dominic's sleepy eyes hardened. "I repeat. Go away, Jules, before I forget you are my brother."

"But, *mon-frère*, I thought that was exactly what you have been trying to forget for the past ten years." At Dominic's silence, Jules leaned across the table, pressing his advantage. "Why have you returned every letter unopened? We were in Brussels at the same time three years ago. When I called at your rooms, your man said you had left the city."

"I did not wish to see you. Then or now," Dominic stated flatly.

"You must listen to me and learn the truth. For the love we once shared. Why can't you see that honor demands it?"

"Honor!" Dominic snarled, leaning close to him. "I have no honor left!"

This time it was Jules who retreated back into the depths of the chair. "Dominic, stop being a fool. You might not have been interested in my whereabouts, but I have followed yours quite closely. You were Wellington's fair-haired boy on the Peninsula. Still are, according to reports, which is probably why Lord Bristol and the Duke of Monmouth have been urging you to take your seat in the House of Lords. You were a hero according to the dispatches."

"Your sources are wrong, Jules. The real heroes died in the stinking mud of the Peninsula." Dominic rose to his feet, but before he could turn away, Jules played his first card.

"I have come back to pay my debt for what happened the night Leticia and Charles died."

Ten years had passed, but his brother's eyes were the same startling blue, colored with pain, that had stared at him across the two newly dug graves.

"You are mad to remind me of that night." Challenge laced Dominic's words as he placed his palms on the table and leaned toward Jules. "You want to talk about that night; the night I discovered that we had not escaped our parent's taint after all." Dominic laughed bitterly. "Yes, I always knew what she was, although you tried to hide it from me. My big brother protecting the young heir from the truth! That my father was a drunk and our mother a wanton who…"

Recoiling from Jules, Dominic stood. "I could even have accepted mother's lovers if I hadn't discovered the real truth. The sins of the parents are visited upon their children. Are they not ... brother? We are our mother's sons ... you proved that to me."

"Am I the excuse for the life you have led the past ten years?" Jules forced his voice to calmness, although he wished to take Dominic and shake him. He had not fully realized how badly scarred his brother had become. Perhaps he had waited too long.

"You are well informed." Dominic's smile was not pleasant. "But I must confess, I have not yet sunk to your depths. Although tonight I made a damn good start!"

All emotion drained from Dominic's face and Jules found he could not meet those eyes, although he could not escape his brother's words.

"Tonight I discovered I am nearly as despicable as you. You see, it does run in the family, after all."

Chapter 8

Juliana pirouetted once in front of the glass, her mauve-figured silk empire gown swirling delicately over the tips of mauve kid slippers. Anticipation colored her cheeks. Tonight's musicale at Lady Atwood's would surely command Dominic's presence. After two days of trying to avoid him, it had been particularly vexing to realize he was nowhere she was. Then at Marcham's Ball, when he had devoted all his attentions to Dora Stanwood, she had been forced to recognize that she meant nothing more than any other woman to him.

The gossips had been quick to whisper of his latest flirt and Lady Grenville had pursed her thin lips, arched her eyebrows, and clucked "Just so", so often than Juliana had retired early with a headache.

Although she admitted to herself that she had fallen in love with Dominic, she was determined not to give herself away. After all, she had Edgemont and Freddie; even Jules had been paying her marked attention. She would enjoy the Season as best she could while trying to untangle her feelings for Dominic.

A soft knock at her door announced Aunt Sophia, who poked her head in. "Juliana, my dear, you look delightful. But we must hurry. Rodney says the crowds are gathering across the square already to gape. And our coachman will have some to negotiate all this traffic."

"Coming, Aunt." Juliana threw the dove gray cape edged in ermine over her shoulders and pulled on mauve elbow-length kid gloves as they descended the staircase.

On their arrival, Rodney escorted Sophia and Juliana, one on each arm, along the length of the Atwood's mirrored ballroom, opened this evening to accommodate the crowd.

"Tout le monde est ici," Lady Atwood fluttered affectedly. "So sorry I was called away from the door before you arrived, but Casper is decidedly absent. The Pignotti's voice does not appeal to him so he's taken the Duke of Clarence, Mortimer D'Espry, and Lord Monmouth to the library for cards."

Rodney seemed to brighten momentarily, but Aunt Sophia sent him a speaking glance and he subsided.

"Ah well," he muttered. "I've always enjoyed the Pignotti, I suppose."

Freddie crossed the floor, took Lady Atwood's hand and lifted it elegantly to his lips for a fleeting kiss. "Charming, as always," he drawled, evoking a muffled giggle from Juliana. He turned and made her an elegant leg.

"Don't try your airs with me, Freddie Liscombe," Juliana hissed.

"You dampen all pretensions, my dear." He turned her away from the others and then in a conspiratorial whisper he continued, "Come with me to the dining room. The lobster pastries are nearly all gone and the footman frowned at me when I went back the last time."

"How many have you had, Freddie?" Juliana questioned merrily.

"Only six. If you're with me, we can pretend you want some."

"But I do, Freddie!" she protested. Being with Freddie was like being with George, she could relax and enjoy all the company around her. When they entered the dining room, she caught sight of the dark visage of Jules and immediately her hand tightened on Freddie's arm. Perhaps if she knew the source of the anger between Jules and his brother she might understand Dominic.

"I promise I won't eat them all, Juliana," Freddie declared, obviously thinking her sudden grip on his arm was her attempt to stop him from reaching for another lobster pastry.

"No need for concern, Freddie. I've quite lost my taste for them. However, a glass of orangeade would be delightful."

With a quick bow, Freddie wove his way through the crush,

but not before he had filched another pastry. Juliana smiled at his retreating back and continued to smile, although it was a bit strained, when Edgemont suddenly stepped in front of her. He appeared quite anxious.

"My dear Juliana, I must speak to you immediately concerning something of the gravest import." "Edgemont, this is such a sad crush. Certainly not the place to discuss anything of import," she soothed, eager to avoid any lengthy discussion with this determined suitor. "You may call on me tomorrow."

His face flushed a deep crimson and his military stance became even more rigid. "Madam, it cannot wait until tomorrow. I must speak to you now." Juliana lifted her chin to deliver a set-down, when over his shoulder she saw Dominic, his golden head haloed by candlelight, his wonderful face radiating mirth, and clinging to his blue velvet covered arm was Dora Stanwood.

"My dear Juliana," Edgemont reiterated. "If you would but give me a few moments of your time. Allow me to remove you from this shocking squeeze."

Yes, away from the sight of Dominic gazing down into Dora's lovely face. Away from the look in Dora's eyes. Is that how I look when I'm gazing at Dominic ... my eyes full of longing and desire.

So she did not protest when Edgemont placed her hand on his sleeve and purposefully moved through the throng. Not until it became suddenly much quieter did she quickly remove her hand and glance around. A latch clicked shut behind her and she twirled to face Edgemont, who was smiling, leaning against the door. They were in a small dimly lit antechamber.

To her horror he fell to his knees, his hand groping toward her. She stepped back, but he did not stop, instead he inched forward on his knees.

"Lord Edgemont, please," she pleaded, backing slowly away from his awkward pursuit.

Finally she reached a small settee and fell into its depths. Edgemont's advance brought his hand to her knee.

"My dearest, dearest," he murmured. "Surely my regard for you has not escaped your notice."

She twitched her knees away. Pressing her palms to suddenly heated cheeks, she shook her head. "My lord! Please rise from that position. I…"

"I know it must seem unbelievable that I could be on my knees to anyone, but, Juliana … may I dare … I wished to show you my great regard…"

"No, my lord…"

"I wished to follow the correct form," he continued without pause. "Always, I do things the correct way."

Juliana's horror had turned to a lively sense of the ridiculous. Perhaps it was just as well to let the man finish, for it seemed nothing she could say would stop him.

"And I am reliably informed," he droned on, "that bending the knee is the proper position for a proposal of marriage."

The door swung wide and Juliana looked up with concern. The interruption should stop Edgemont, but she hated to have him caught by anyone like this. Framed in the doorway, blotting out the hallway beyond, stood Dominic.

Juliana's sense of the ridiculous fled. Mortified beyond words, she could only sit, stunned while Edgemont rose to his feet protesting this invasion of privacy.

Dominic turned slightly. "You see, my dear," he said clearly, "even people of the first respectability use these chambers for a … respite from the crowd. Unfortunately," his lips curled into a sneer, "this one is already occupied."

Dora peeped around the corner and dimpled coyly. "It appears we may have interrupted a conversation of import."

"Ah, Juliana, there you are." Jules entered the room and extended his hand. "Your aunt sent me to fetch you."

He pulled her to her feet and escorted her past a sputtering Edgemont to the doorway, where briefly she met Dominic's icy blue stare.

"I'm sure you all will excuse us," the Comte purred softly.

Gratefully, Juliana allowed Jules to lead her back into the lights and noise of the Atwood musicale, still wondering at his timely appearance.

"I am sorry I did not arrive sooner, but Lady Sefton

waylaid me."

Her eyes flew to his face. "But how did you know I needed rescuing?"

"Your thoughts were obviously elsewhere or you never would have allowed Edgemont to maneuver you into that tiny antechamber. Which, of course, is for the sole purpose of clandestine meetings."

"No wonder Dominic was bringing Dora there," she fumed aloud.

He led her to a choice seat near Aunt Sophia. "Yes, one never knows what truly motivates my younger brother. You, of all people, should realize that." He smiled enigmatically into her stunned face.

Then his gaze lifted across the entire width of the ballroom. Involuntarily Juliana followed that gaze and saw Dominic glowering at them from his position at the windows.

She felt confused by Jules's attentions, as if in some unknown way she was being disloyal to Dominic. But he was a decided comfort, and it was reassuring to have such an eligible party take her up in such a particular way. She knew, deep in her heart, that Jules had no romantic feeling for her, but she refused to believe he was using her as an instrument of revenge. She felt she could trust her judgment at least that far. Edgemont seemed to have disappeared for the rest of the evening, but Freddie, mercifully, appeared to lead her in for the Pignotti's recital. She understood Lord Atwood's preference for the card room when the piercing high notes caused goose bumps to raise on her arm.

She turned to Freddie to share her amusement and found he was lost in rapt admiration of the singer. Shaking her head slightly, there was no accounting for taste, she scanned the music room. Her eyes caught and held Dominic's and for a moment they shared that odd sense of understanding.

Then she noticed Lord Monmouth beckon to him. All of her pleasure in the evening disappeared through the doorway with him.

• • •

Juliana opened her eyes to the sound of rain against her window. It was early for there were no sounds of household activity and no one had as yet knocked at her door with morning chocolate. Not wishing to go back to sleep, she sat up, plumping her pillows and settling against them.

Between the gap of her window curtains she could see the trees bent with the wind, sending raindrops swirling through the air. It was a dreadful day, a day to sit in front of a cozy fire with someone.

She couldn't help herself today, any more than she could any morning for the past week, from thinking of Dominic. She imagined several delightful scenes where Dominic came begging her forgiveness before sweeping her up in his arms, declaring that he loved her and raining his marvelous kisses about her person. These were childish daydreams, she knew. It was better that he had stayed away, for it had given her time to come to grips with the love she felt for him.

Sitting up, she pushed back the bedcovers. She hadn't decided what her best course was to be yet, but she would simply stop thinking about him and keep herself very, very busy about the house.

That afternoon Juliana interrupted a heated conversation between her aunt and Lord Rodney in the parlor.

"Oh dear," Juliana said, embarrassed. "I didn't mean to intrude, I thought you'd be in the morning room as usual."

"Don't be absurd," Aunt Sophia smiled. "Rodney and I are only having a small discussion, aren't we dear?"

Lord Rodney looked into his teacup as if wishing it to be the devil. He suddenly stood with a determined look on his face. Juliana was surprised to discover that he was actually getting thinner.

"No, we were not having a small discussion. We were having our first disagreement. And it concerns you, Juliana."

"Me!" She glanced at her aunt who was gazing at Rodney's purposeful stance, a curious smile hovering about her mouth.

"How masterful, dear, I'm quite impressed."

"Damn it, Sophia! I mean it. You are coming to Culter

Towers with Dominic and me. Their graces are eager to meet you."

Again Juliana looked from her aunt, calmly sitting on the couch, to Lord Rodney, who had begun to pace about the room. She sank down next to Sophia trying to interpret the meaning of this strange pronouncement.

"Of course, you must go, Aunt Sophia. How exciting for you!"

Her aunt looked at her in surprise. "I can't possible leave you here alone. How could you even think it?"

Smiling complacently, Rodney rocked back on his heels. "No need for worry, my dear. I have the solution, Juliana shall come with us."

"What an excellent idea," Sophia said eagerly, casting an adoring look at his lordship.

"Oh, no, I couldn't possibly…" She stopped when two pairs of determined eyes stared at her. Then she attempted to go on. "I am honored, of course, to meet the Duke and Duchess of Culter, but … George … I couldn't possibly leave before George even arrives in town."

As if on cue the parlor doors were flung open.

"Master George!" Smithers announced loudly.

"Cut line, Smithers," her brother said, grinning. "They know who I am."

"George!" Juliana and Sophia chorused at once, before both rushed forward to fall about his neck.

"Good God, you're both strangling me," he laughed merrily, placing loud kisses on both their cheeks before untangling himself to make a formal bow to Rodney.

"Your servant, sir. I am George Vane."

Gliding over to his lordship, Aunt Sophia placed a light hand on his arm. "George, dear, I'd like you to meet Lord Rodney Crawford. My betrothed."

George's mouth dropped open but he quickly recovered. "Aunt Sophia, I don't know what to say."

"Wish me happy." Laughing, Sophia flung out her arms and George gathered her in a warm embrace. She looked at Juliana, whose evident confusion delighted her.

"So that's what this is all about. I should have guessed. Aunt Sophia, I'm so happy for you."

George stood back measuring Lord Rodney for just an instant before extending one hand to him. "Sir, you are a fortunate man."

Juliana, charmed by the proud look on Lord Rodney's face, was gratified to hear him answer, "I know I am, my boy. Can't quite believe my good fortune myself!"

"Please, you will both put me to the blush," laughed Sophia, steering George to the master wing chair facing the fireplace. "I'm sure you need something to wash the dust from your throat. Juliana, will you ring for Bella. We all could use some tea."

"I'm sure George would like some brandy," Juliana retorted. She crossed to the bellpull and tugged, sending the silent message to the kitchens that Bella was summoned. As she passed George's chair, she leaned down to drop a kiss upon his rich auburn curls.

He caught her hand, bringing it to his lips, a twinkle in his eyes. "Ah, how I've missed my beautiful sister. I trust I've not lost you to cupid's arrow just yet, have I?"

Carefully avoiding Aunt Sophia's eyes, Juliana smiled slowly. "Of course not, my dear, you are still stuck with me."

"So, George, you know about the pl ... huh!" sputtered Rodney as Sophia trod heavily upon his foot.

"Sorry, my dear, I was reaching for my shawl," Sophia said serenely, placing it about her shoulders. "Yes, George, we are enjoying the Season. But we plan to be away for a few weeks at Culter Towers visiting Rodney's parents, the duke and duchess. We hope you and Juliana will join us."

Before her brother could respond, Juliana laughed lightly, placing her hands lovingly upon his shoulders. "George has only just arrived, Aunt Sophia. We don't want to rush him away from town before he can sample its pleasures."

Twining his fingers through hers, George looked up at her. "Actually, Juliana, you're right. Wouldn't mind cards at White's."

"White's! Delighted for you to be my guest..." Rodney

glanced warily at Sophia's slipper moving dangerously close to his boot again. "Let's take in White's. If you're not too tired from your journey."

Sophia sprang up. "How delightful for you, George. You know how you love your cards."

Before Juliana quite realized what was happening, Aunt Sophia was maneuvering both men from the parlor. "Yes, you mustn't miss this opportunity, George. Juliana and I shall stay at home this evening and have a light supper." Peeking back into the parlor, Sophia's face glowed. "You see, Juliana," she whispered. "The plan is working."

After seeing Aunt Sophia settled in her room with a light supper, Juliana wandered through the downstairs rooms, absentmindedly touching a few treasured pieces: the Sevres vase her mother had received as a betrothal gift, the ormolu clock her grandfather supposedly won in a wager over a horse race, the Faberge egg an adventuring great-uncle had brought back from his travels. She stopped in front of the Reynolds portrait of her father hung prominently over the parlor fireplace.

"Well Papa," she whispered to the laughing man whose hand rested on his favorite hound, "I've brought George here at last. Maybe he'll learn to enjoy life a little more while we're here … maybe we all will."

She turned and lit the candle at the fireside chair, then settled into it. Lord Rodney had taken George to White's for the evening, and she had sent a messenger declining Edgemont's card party, so for once, she faced a quiet evening alone.

A short space found her restlessly moving about the room again, finally ending at the window to stare out into St. James Square. The lamps had been lit, casting oddly shaped shadows onto the paving bricks. Carriages whisked by, and the *ton* rushed to this evening's entertainment. What would Dominic do? Perhaps a party … gambling with friends … Vauxhall … no, not Vauxhall. Maybe he would visit Dora, or one of the fashionable impures he was rumored to be so popular with. Leaning her forehead against a cool pane, she closed her eyes. At least she had an excuse for staying in London now and a suitable chaperon in George. The longer she could postpone meeting the marquis again, the better.

Dominic discovered his uncle seated in a corner near one of the curtained window dormers of the lounge at White's. Rodney was gazing into his brandy glass, a satisfied smile on his face.

Dominic sat in the deep wing chair opposite him. "You look pleased with yourself, Uncle."

"So I am, dear boy, so I am!" Draining the last of his brandy, Rodney put down his glass and sat back. "Sophia will be going to Culter Towers with us. Juliana's brother has arrived in town so now she has no excuse. You must meet the lad, you'll like him."

"I have and I do," Dominic laughed. "Came across him with Freddie in the card room. Obviously George is as an inveterate player as Freddie. They seem to have taken a liking to one another."

"Yes. Sophia will be delighted." He chuckled, a besotted look descending upon his features. "Pleased her this afternoon, too. I suggested that Juliana go to the Towers with us. Perhaps she still should. We could bring George and make it a real house party." He clasped his hands across his diminishing stomach and eyed Dominic. "What do you think, my boy? It would relieve the tedium of having the Grenvilles. Can't imagine what your grandmother's thinking of, inviting them. Eugenia Grenville hasn't been there since you were an infant. I can't understand the sudden interest." Dominic started to tell his uncle why the Grenvilles had been invited but then stopped, thinking better of it. After all, he might be misjudging his grandmother, although he doubted it. She had warned him that now he was nine and twenty it was time to settle down and produce an heir, which meant he had to find a wife. What had been her exact words? Something about parading every eligible chit in front of him until he found one he would wed. Or more correctly, one that would overlook his reputation for a crown of strawberry leaves. She had obviously decided to start with distant family relatives.

"Invite them both if you like." Dominic shrugged.

"Although George may not want to leave the pleasures of London, since he's so recently arrived. I'm thinking of staying in town myself."

His uncle sat bolt upright. "You can't do that to me! Your grandmother will stir quite a fuss if you don't show up. Sent me a long detailed letter about how I was to be sure you didn't disappoint the duke again. You know she has the devil's own temper."

"Grandfather will keep her in line."

"He's even worse. Never raises his voice, but somehow makes me feel I'm back at Eton. Can't expect me to face them both without you. I promised!"

Dominic frowned. Juliana at Culter Towers, seeing her every day. He hadn't been able to keep his hands off her at Vauxhall, and if anything, his feelings seemed to be growing stronger. To think he had once thought he could find someone worthy of her. There was no one. Especially not himself! How he must disgust her. He had treated her like all the others and she was not. She was … NO! He must close the door on those thoughts.

He raised his hand and instantly a waiter appeared with a brandy glass. He tipped the entire contents down his throat before answering his uncle. God forgive him for wanting her and knowing in his heart that she felt drawn to him. He had misled Jules, he still had enough honor to lay awake night after night recalling vividly the reasons why Juliana could never, under any circumstances, become a part of his life. Drawing upon what pride remained to him, he made his decision. Aware of Rodney's worried look, he smiled faintly.

"Wouldn't do that to you, old boy. Invite Juliana and George. If Her Grace desires a house party, we shall give her one … Come, let's play a hand of piquet."

As they moved away from the window enclosure, one long white finger parted the curtain slightly. Satisfied that no one was watching, Jules stepped quickly into the center of the lounge, crossed to the servant's hall, and disappeared.

• • •

Smither's knock roused Juliana from the air dreams she had been spinning.

"Why it's quite dark. Light the chandelier, please, Smithers?"

"Yes, my lady. You have a caller." He hesitated slightly. "A gentleman."

Dominic. Her hands flew to her hair unconsciously straightening any stray wisps. She fought to keep her breathing under control as she answered softly. "Show him in."

The room was lit softly with only the high chandelier and the fireplace burning. The drapes had been drawn and suddenly the parlor seemed a small, cozy room. Juliana stood and glanced quickly into the gilt mirror. Yes, she would do.

"The Comte de Saville, ma'am."

Light-headed with disappointment, Juliana fought to compose herself, holding out one hand in welcome. Jules bent over it carefully.

"Please be seated, my lord."

"Jules."

"Smithers, I'd like a tea tray. My ... Jules, would you care for something stronger?"

"Tea will be fine. You were expecting someone else?"

Juliana turned swiftly and crossed to the chair by the fire. "No, I have been enjoying a rare night of quiet." She smoothed her gown self-consciously. "I am curious, however, why you have called so late."

"My dear Juliana," Jules began smoothly, "I heard the news about Rodney and Sophia."

"Yes?"

His eye narrowed slightly and he half turned from her direct gaze. "Of course, I wished to offer my felicitations."

"Unfortunately neither of them is here to receive your kind thoughts." For some reason, here in her own parlor, Juliana felt uncomfortable and knew a need to challenge every statement Jules made.

"Yes, I know." Jules's thin lips quirked at the corners. "I just left Rodney and Dominic at White's. We were discussing the house party you will be joining at Culter Towers. The duke and duchess are most eager to meet Sophia and her family."

"Sophia is also looking forward to making their acquaintance. However, you are mistaken. George and I will not be in attendance," she stated firmly.

Jules cast her a long, cool stare before he shrugged, frowning, "I am sorry you will not be there to give Sophia your support."

"My support?" she responded quickly. "My dear Comte, Sophia will charm the Duke and Duchess of Culter as quickly as she has Rodney."

Jules laughed, his one eye sparkling yet brittle. "Rodney is indeed besotted with your aunt. But their graces can be difficult at best. Especially when it concerns the continuation of their line."

Slight as it had been, Juliana caught and understood Jules's inference to her aunt's age. "Are you saying that the duke and duchess are displeased because Rodney has chosen a mature woman instead of a chit right out of the schoolroom?" she asked with false civility.

Jules spread out his hands before settling more comfortably upon the sofa. "All who know her, value Sophia's uniqueness. In time, I'm sure…"

"In time!" Juliana interrupted, exasperated past bearing with the condescending tone of the Comte's voice. "If Rodney … and their graces … searched through all of time and beyond, they could find no one more worthy than Aunt Sophia!"

She was trembling in anger, her protective instincts toward her beloved aunt raised to a fever pitch.

Suddenly leaning forward, Jules clasped her shaking fingers in his warm hand. "Juliana, it was not my intention to upset you. It was simply my wish to encourage you to join Sophia at the Towers."

He released her suddenly stilled fingers and the expression in his dark face showed only concern. "We would … all … miss you at the Towers." Jules watched her stand and cross to the fire, taking a poker to jab at the smothering log. Her profile was lit by the low flame, so he knew the moment when she made her decision.

"Perhaps I have been too hasty," Juliana considered out loud, her chin lifting in determination. "My brother has only just arrived in London. We shall give it a few days before deciding ... it was ... thoughtful of you to be concerned, sir."

When she turned her attention to the refreshment tray, he could not stop his mouth from curling into a satisfied smile. He had come to realize that through this woman his debt to Dominic could be paid.

Chapter 9

The Duke of Culter had sent his own luxurious traveling coach to convey the party to the Towers. Juliana, seated across from Lady Grenville, thought she looked like a cat that had just finished a particularly large dish of cream. Aunt Sophia wore her usually calm expression, although her lips did twitch now and again when she glanced at Eugenia. The fourth occupant of the carriage, Sir Alfred, kept his mouth shut, hiding behind his copy of the *Times*, just as always. Sometimes one *did* forget that he was even there. She leaned back, trying to ease a small ache in her lower back and gazed longingly out the window. Charlotte and George rode side by side, totally engrossed in conversation. How nice it would be to be out in the sunshine, riding with a pleasant companion in the fresh air of the countryside.

Dominic, astride Bucephalus, cut off her view. On second thought, it was better to be stuck in this stifling carriage than be out there with him.

There should be a law against Dominic on horseback. The effect was devastating to Juliana's peace of mind. Dressed in magnificently cut pearl gray riding clothes, he was a veritable Adonis on his white charger, sweeping all before him. No wonder rumor credited him with so many hearts. And, she was no different than the rest. She, too, had fallen victim to his legendary charm.

The problem was how to deal with it. She had had to come on this trip, especially after Jules's cryptic remark about Aunt Sophia's reception by the duke and duchess. She fumed inwardly. No one would be allowed to say a word against her beloved aunt. Why, they should be happy that Rodney had found such a prize!

Early that morning as they had gathered at Wentworth

House for the journey to the Towers, Dominic had greeted her carefully, showing her only the degree of kindness he did Charlotte. And he had approved heartily of her traveling in the carriage. Perhaps because Juliana loved him, she sensed a constraint in him that had not been there before. They were both so polite. Too polite. Did he never think of Vauxhall? Had he no further desire to enfold her in his arms as he had that night? Her thoughts centered on that moment in the ruin, and a delicious shiver caused her to pull her light cashmere shawl tighter around her shoulders. Those memories were so precious ... if only she knew what to do ... what Dominic was thinking. It was difficult feeling her way through all the emotions surrounding her. It hadn't been this way with Will, love had seemed so simple, so easy. With Dominic nothing was easy, and she had no guidelines to follow. She sorted through each precious memory of Dominic—the haughty autocrat was gone, replaced by the tender man of the ruin of Mrs. Forbes's garden.

Unbidden, she thought of a gnarled hand pressing against her chest. Go with your feelings, Mrs. Forbes had told her. And she had seemed infinitely wise. But if Juliana acted on her feelings, she would go against all that society expected. And if she risked that much, where would it lead? She sighed softly and tucked her head against the cushion propped in the corner.

Juliana's sigh pulled Sophia out of her reverie. If only Rodney hadn't gone ahead with Jules. If he were here, he would keep them all delightfully entertained with his stories. Then Sir Alfred wouldn't have to doze behind his paper hoping to avoid his wife's censure, and Juliana wouldn't be frowning in apparent concentration, and Eugenia wouldn't be plotting whatever stratagems she had concocted to bring Charlotte to Dominic's notice. Sophia was nearly ill with worry. She noticed the strain between Juliana and Dominic, had sensed its beginnings at Vauxhall. Something had happened to those two that night. Juliana had looked as if she would shatter into a thousand pieces if anyone had touched her. And Dominic ... Sophia feared nothing and no one, but the look on his face had chilled her. At the same time she wept inwardly for him.

The picture Rodney had revealed of his life was not pretty. His was a complex, perhaps even dark personality, but she had seen flashes of an inner spirit and warmth in his dealings with Juliana. She was trusting her vaunted intuition totally. If anyone could touch him, it was her precious niece. She only hoped she would not be sorry later.

Culter Towers came into view late in the afternoon. Down a long avenue of silver beech trees the twin stone towers rose against a glorious red sunset.

"My goodness, it's magnificent," Aunt Sophia remarked, sticking her head out the window.

"I know you're not accustomed to such grandeur, Sophia," Lady Grenville sniffed, "but do try not to act the rustic."

"Eugenia, my dear, how kind of you to be concerned," Aunt Sophia said in a dangerously soft voice. "But truly there is no need. Rodney has assured me that the duke and duchess will find me enchanting … after all … I shall soon be their daughter."

The red fan that Lady Grenville had used constantly during their journey snapped in two pieces as a horrible scarlet stained her cheeks.

"You think you're so clever, don't you!" her ladyship spit out between clenched teeth. "But I shall best you. Charlotte will be the next duchess, not you!"

Juliana, shocked into silence by Lady Grenville's viciousness, wondered at her aunt's confidence. Jules had hinted Sophia might not be so graciously received, but she clearly had no doubts. Her merry laughter sang through the coach, instantly dispelling the charged atmosphere and causing Sir Alfred to snore slightly as he automatically shifted back farther into his corner.

"Don't be ridiculous, Eugenia. I have no desire to be a duchess and neither, I believe, does Charlotte."

"And Juliana? I certainly hope you have no aspirations for Juliana in that direction, because we both know they won't allow the heir to wed another widow. After the disas…"

"That is quite enough!" her aunt hissed.

"Aunt Sophia…" Juliana began, but stopped when her aunt shook her head.

Juliana sat stiffly upright, startled by this strange revelation. What was going on here? A knot formed in her chest, right over her heart, at the guilty look on her aunt's face. Her eyes were steadily avoiding Juliana's. She clenched her hands in her lap, schooling her own face to reveal nothing.

The coach lurched to a stop on the cobbled courtyard before the sweeping stone steps where Rodney waited eagerly. Jules stood a little behind him, smiling faintly when Juliana stepped from the carriage.

Lady Grenville bustled Sir Alfred right up the steps past Rodney, as if he were totally unimportant, to the great carved door where the duke and duchess waited.

Rodney embraced Sophia lightly and nodded welcomingly to Juliana before escorting his fiancée up the stairs. George and Charlotte came racing from the stables, laughing together, interrupting any chance of private speech Juliana may have wanted with Jules.

"Dominic's seeing to the horses." George took a girl on each arm and mounted the steps. Juliana hesitated, turning to Jules, her eyes questioning, but he merely inclined his head, smiling, and stepped aside so they might ascend to where the Duke and Duchess of Culter awaited them.

The duchess was nothing like she had expected. Small and finely boned, with beautiful, nearly translucent skin, she looked sweet and fragile, unlike the haughty duchess of her imagination. On the other hand, the duke was exactly as she had envisioned. She now knew what Dominic would look like in his seventies, tall and straight, with a mane of pure white hair. Austin Crawford, the eighth Duke of Culter, was in his own way breathtaking, especially when he suddenly looked at her with the same cornflower blue eyes as Dominic.

"And this is the beautiful Juliana." His voice was strong and deep as he lifted her fingers to his lips. "Welcome to Culter Towers, my dear."

Her eyes searched his face and found nothing but welcome for her, for Aunt Sophia … what had Jules meant by his remarks concerning Sophia? Then over the duke's shoulder she saw

Dominic move to kiss his grandmother. What secrets did this family share? What had Lady Grenville meant by her cutting remark? And more importantly, why had Aunt Sophia looked so distressed?

Juliana had little time to pursue these thoughts for the duchess, with much graciousness plus a large dose of firmness, sent everyone to their chambers.

Her room was an enormous garden: flower print of pink, periwinkle blue, and cream covered every inch of wall, curtained the bed, and covered the windows. A footman promptly appeared with hot water in huge jars. He crossed to a small room and pulled a copper hip bath in front of the fireplace, which he filled without speaking a word.

Immediately a diminutive young country girl, with a mop of glossy, daffodil yellow curls, appeared with lavender-scented towels. "Me name is Mary, and I'm to be your lady's maid during your stay, miss." She smiled saucily at the footman and hurried him out of the room before opening a bottle of scented oil and carefully adding a few drops to the steaming bathwater. "There. That will be ever so nice for you, miss. I have scented soap for your hair. I'll place the towels just here by the fire so they will be nice and warm. What else would you like, miss? I'm ever so happy to be here to serve you."

"I'm pleased to have you, Mary. I'm quite lost without my maid." Juliana didn't feel the slightest twinge of remorse for telling such a white lie, because Mary was so eager that she couldn't have told the child she nearly always dressed herself.

She was rewarded by a beaming smile and a constantly chattering tongue. During Juliana's bath she learned that Mary had just finished her training and she was her first lady, that Mary had seven brothers and sisters on one of the home farms, that Ma was poorly after the last baby, so all the older kids had gone into service to help out "exceptin" Thomas. Master Dominic got him into the navy as a cabin boy to a ol' school friend, Master Dominic says will look after him. "Imagine that!"

Juliana sat in front of the fire pulling a silver brush through her damp curls, smiling and nodding occasionally to encourage the young maid, but her mind was stayed on Dominic and the secret she would have to coax her aunt to share.

"Ooh, miss. This would be ever so pretty with your hair." Mary was holding up a jade green satin evening gown Juliana had never worn. "And real proper for dinner tonight. Her Grace always dresses every so grand. Even when it's just her and the duke. She'll be a right proper duchess with a house party and all."

When Juliana had rested, been dressed in the shimmering evening gown, and had her hair becomingly styled by an unexpectedly talented Mary, she went in search of her aunt. She stood outside Sophia's room looking up and down the corridor, feeling rather foolish hovering about, but she could hear voices from the bedchamber, and what she had to ask Aunt Sophia required privacy.

At last the door opened, but it was not the maid leaving. Aunt Sophia, resplendent in a cream silk gown with a gold satin overskirt, sailed out, followed by Lord Rodney.

"Juliana!" gasped Sophia, caught unaware. She looked radiant. There was a new light in her eyes and in Rodney's.

He immediately placed an arm about Sophia's shoulders. "You startled us, my dear Juliana," he began with great dignity. "I have just had the honor of presenting the Crawford betrothal ring to your aunt."

With a wide smile, Sophia held out her hand upon which she now wore a huge emerald surrounded by a blaze of diamonds. "Isn't it beautiful?"

Tears misted Juliana's eyes. "Lovely," she breathed, before kissing both on their cheeks. "I'm so happy that you two have found each other again."

Rodney offered an arm to Juliana while holding out his hand to Sophia. "What luck to be escorting the two loveliest ladies here to dinner."

They entered the drawing room where the duke and duchess awaited their guests. Rodney drew Sophia to the large wing chair and again formally presented her. Juliana watched the interplay carefully, searching for signs of disapproval, but could see none. The duchess, dressed in black silk with diamonds sparkling at her throat, ears, and wrists, welcomed Sophia openly and warmly. She lifted one eyebrow and spoke Rodney's name in a tone that must have caused terror in the schoolroom.

He immediately lifted Sophia's hand so the blaze of diamonds and emeralds could reflect the light.

Her Grace appeared relieved. "Ah, I see this will be a celebration dinner!" She beckoned to Rodney and he leaned down to receive a congratulatory kiss.

"I shall do my best to make him happy, Your Grace," Sophia remarked solemnly.

"I have no doubt you will succeed." Turning a stern eye to her youngest son, she studied him from the tips of his evening slippers to the top of his carefully combed dark curls. "He already looks better than he has in years. I believe he has even been able to give up his corse…"

"Rodney, my boy! We are delighted for you!" the duke interrupted. "I never thought to have such a beautiful daughter." He cupped Sophia's face in his hands as if she were a young girl. She responded with her particularly appealing smile. "Enchanting," he murmured before kissing her cheek.

"Grandfather always arrives in the nick of time," whispered Dominic, his breath softly stirring Juliana's curls. "Remember, I told you Mrs. Forbes's outspoken ways reminded me of my own grandmother."

When had he come in? She'd been so engrossed in Rodney and Sophia, she hadn't felt his presence. She turned slowly to face him. The candlelight lit golden and red highlights in his hair and cast intriguing shadows across the planes of his face. He was smiling at her, the first real smile in days, and she forced her breath to remain steady.

"I remember it well, Dominic. As I do all our meetings … although some have been more memorable than others."

Now, why had she said that—for the satisfaction of seeing surprise flicker through his eyes? Perhaps he'd forgotten Vauxhall, when for once he hadn't denied his need for her, but she never would. It had been a turning point for her, and now she very much feared all her happiness depended on him.

She shouldn't have reminded him. Dominic's eyes, that had sparkled with vitality, went curiously blank and the closeness of the moment before was gone.

"Tonight should be memorable, for we've discovered we shall soon be cousins," he said lightly. Then he looked at Rodney and Sophia accepting hearty congratulations from George and Charlotte. "He appears to be very happy tonight. I hope he remains that way."

Before she could answer, he walked away. Frustrated, she wanted to follow. Why should he question Rodney and Sophia's happiness? Why did every attempt to bring him closer just push him farther away? He had approached Lady Grenville, and Juliana was reluctant to confront her until she had learned more about her mysterious statement in the carriage.

Dearborne, the butler, announced dinner. Dominic offered his arm to Charlotte—a gesture that drew warm smiles from his grandmother and her mother, but thoughtful frowns from George and the duke.

Although the vaulted ceiling of the great dining hall cast dark shadows, the room had a festive air. A large fire blazed in the hearth and two six-branched candelabra lit the long, polished table. Candles burned on the mantel and on the sideboard from which Dearborne supervised the serving of their dinner.

By the time the company had sampled potage St. Germaine, the *fruits de mer* platter, and started on the rack of veal, Juliana was wishing for her room. She had the unenviable position in the middle of the table, flanked by George and Lady Grenville, and facing Lord Grenville. She envied her aunt the position at the duke's right, for laughter could be heard often at their end of the table. No one ignored her precisely, but most often she suffered through Lady Grenville's boring monologue. Juliana now knew all of Lady Grenville's connections to the Crawfords, the age and partial history of the Towers, even the size of the stone in the heir's betrothal ring, which she made sure Juliana realized was larger and more valuable than the one presented to Aunt Sophia.

Lady Grenville had smirked when relating this little tidbit and cast an indulgent eye at Charlotte who was leaning eagerly across the table to talk to George. "Normally," she informed Juliana, "Charlotte would be taken to task for this indiscretion, but since this a family party, strict social rules can be relaxed somewhat."

And Juliana mused, it was an opportunity for Charlotte to display her interest in and knowledge of country matters. In fact, she and George were discussing the merits of draining the east four hundred acres near the creek, which divided the Park from the Willows. Never before had she realized how much they had in common.

At least they were enjoying themselves! If Sir Alfred hadn't been directly across from her, she would have parted the flower arrangement to begin a new conversation, but with him it would do no good—she had never heard him offer an opinion on anything, and Lady Grenville would probably answer her anyway.

She could not see Jules, but she could sometimes hear snatches of his charming banter with the duchess. Only Dominic seemed to share her discomfort. Every time she glanced his way, which was more often than she should, he was wearing that blank look, or worse, a frown. Sometime tonight she must talk to Aunt Sophia. Perhaps if she knew more about this secret, she could find the right direction to reach through the barriers he'd built around himself.

The duchess rose gracefully, waggling her fingers at Sophia. "Come, my dear, we'll have a comfortable coze while the gentlemen tell their stories." She waited until Lady Grenville had ponderously risen from her chair, still wiping the remains of the last sweet from her fingers, then led all the ladies into the music room across the hall. At a speaking glance from her mother Charlotte went straight to the pianoforte and exclaimed over it.

"Please feel free to play, Charlotte. It is always delightful to have music after dinner." The Duchess settled onto the settee, inviting Lady Grenville and Sophia to join her.

Juliana wandered toward the doors overlooking a flagstone terrace. She opened one a crack and breathed in the sweetness of the summer evening. Grateful for a few moments of peace, she collected herself before the men joined them and she would be faced with Dominic's intrusive presence. Everything reflected him—a snatch of conversation would remind her of words they had shared; the duke would smile and she'd see Dominic's mouth laughing. She longed to share in the atmosphere of love and security that surrounded Rodney and Sophia, yet knew her own unhappiness barred the way. She felt so alone.

Jules had befriended her in London, but he was no help here. He hung back from the party, almost as if he were waiting for something. Dominic's brooding presence filtered into all her thoughts, compelling her to look at him, but he would always turn away. Then she'd turn to Jules's face to find he was watching them. There was nothing there to help her.

The slight breeze lifted a curl at the back of her neck and she turned to watch Sophia. The duchess was happily explaining Crawford wedding traditions. She sighed. Jules had certainly misled her. There hadn't been a sign that Sophia was resented or unwelcome. Juliana needn't have come. She could have stayed in London and spared herself.

Footsteps in the hallway roused the duchess to ring for tea. Discouraged and in no mood to deal with Dominic, Juliana signaled to Aunt Sophia that she was going out to the garden for a few moments. She slipped through the doorway and out onto the terrace as the men entered the room.

Walking down a crushed rock path through carefully designed flower beds and neatly trimmed hedges, she could feel the tension drain out of her. The path turned and she decided to follow it to the end. A small cul-de-sac held a marble statue of a shepherd with a lamb curled in sleep at his feet. She sat on the bench and gently ran a finger over the lamb's head. The stone felt cold. Madame Bretin's lovely gown was not practical for walking in the cool of an English night. She shivered and placed her palms over her bare shoulders.

"Shall I fetch your shawl?" A deep male voice spoke from the shadows.

She gasped in surprise when Dominic stepped out into the moonlight. A trembling started in the region of her stomach and threatened to overpower her. Now that she was finally alone with him again, the first time since Vauxhall, she was consumed with uncertainty. Follow her heart … she dare not be so bold.

"Thank you, no, I am quite comfortable," she replied softly, folding her trembling hand into the pleats of her evening gown.

He looked at her bent head, the shadow between her breasts, and, as always, he felt the urge to touch her. Instead he sat on the bench beside her. For a few moments he could sit with her in the peace of this lovely night.

Perhaps, he would even find the words he needed to explain that night at Vauxhall. He had seen the confusion and hurt in her eyes and somehow he must remove that look. For Juliana's sake, they needed to talk about what had happened between them. Then they both could forget it. The fault had been his. He had lost control, as if he were a lovesick boy. But tonight he had not drunk too much. Tonight he was in control. Tonight it would be all right to sit close like this for just a few moments more.

"We seem to meet in out of the way places, Juliana. You should be more careful where you stroll alone."

Her head came up abruptly, the look of pain and confusion again in her eyes.

"You have not made it easy for me to thank you … regardless of what occurred between us … I owe you much for finding me that night."

"You owe me nothing." His voice sounded hoarse to his own ears. "I shouldn't have touched you that night. You're too fine, too perfect…" He caught himself. "I do apologize for my advances. Please forgive me."

Her eyes looked at him in mute appeal.

What did she want from him? To be here in the garden at his own home with her was a fantasy. He never would have believed it could happen, yet here she was and he found he could not bear it. Abruptly he stood to go.

"Dominic," she reached a trembling hand toward him and stood so that they were close. So very close that her scent filled his senses.

She's still cold, he told himself, the trembling means she's cold. Yet he could not resist taking her gently into his arms, even though he knew it was wrong.

"You're cold, my dear. We should go in."

Her trembling had transferred itself to him. They stood together for an eternity before he shifted her slowly in his arms so that he could bring his lips down onto her soft mouth. He had to do it. Just one more time he had to feel her melt into his embrace. Fingers gently molding her arms, he kissed her again. A soft sigh, a sweet breath released into his mouth. His kiss hardened and his arms moved lower to encircle her waist.

He was a lovesick boy! Carefully he put her away from him, separating their bodies. If he didn't stop now, he would carry her into the nearest flower bed and love her as he had been longing to do since they first met.

"We had best return to the others, Juliana. We shall be missed." He had to protect her from himself. As much as he longed to stay out here in the starry night with her, honor demanded that he return to the safety of the house immediately.

She was dreaming. Dominic wasn't really here. It was just a dream she had concocted sitting alone in the night. She reached her hand to his cheek and was surprised when he backed away. What had she done now?

He offered her his arm politely and drew her back down the path toward the house. Her fingers rode lightly over his muscle; it was clenched as if a great struggle was going on within him. They both were silent and too soon the lights from the house were visible.

All the party was gathered around the tea tray except George, who was choosing music for Charlotte to resume playing. Jules turned first at their entrance, a glint of steel in his face. He lifted an eyebrow but said nothing.

Sophia's artless laugh filled the room. "Did you enjoy your walk in the garden? Rodney tells me the grounds here are lovely," she turned to the duchess, "and all to your design."

Lady Grenville opened her mouth but the duke, again, intervened. "Dominic, my boy. I wish to discuss Bristol's and Monmouth's plan for you to join the House of Lords. Wonderful idea, don't you think?"

Juliana smiled at the duke's eager face before turning to Dominic. Swallowing hard, she willed her heartbeat to slow down. "Thank you for the tour of the garden," she said quite distinctly. "All that fresh air has tired me, I believe I'll go up to my room now."

She wanted to be alone to savor the miracle. Dominic had kissed her again. Surely everyone in the room could see it plainly on her face.

Suddenly he stepped to block her path, bending toward her. "Not too tired to ride with me tomorrow." He spoke so softly that only she could hear. "I promise you a horse worthy of your talent, sired by Bucephalus."

She was unable to resist his conspiratorial whisper, and the light she saw in his eyes sent shivers of excitement through her. "I'd love to ride with you."

"Ten o'clock. Don't be late."

Juliana slipped out before Lady Grenville could corner her. The tall clock was chiming softly in the hall as she mounted the steps to her chamber. Never before had she felt so many conflicting emotions. Glorious, wonderful delight! He had kissed her again. It was really quite simple. She loved him, when he was with her all was perfect. And he had invited her to ride with him alone. Maybe here at his home, away from the city, he would tell her what had been troubling him. Maybe tomorrow they could resolve all that stood between them. She felt no shame that she desired him so, so much that there in the garden she would have been willing to lie with him among the flowers, if he had asked her. Whatever fear or convention had stopped her at Vauxhall would not stop her again. She was sure of it, sure at last of the rightness of her love for Dominic.

Drifting off to sleep, she remembered Mrs. Forbes. I'm doing it ... I'm following my heart ... where will it all lead?

The hall clock chimed twelve times and, sighing, Dominic turned away from the windows. Why had he asked her to ride alone with him? Was he trying to prove that he could do the decent thing? That he could be a congenial host. In the daylight it would be easier to be with her—to explain that his high regard for her would remain just that. It could lead to nothing else a gently bred lady might expect. He could not reach out to Will Grenville's young wife.

Regret for the last ten years darkened his thoughts. Regret for what he had allowed himself to become. Jules, at least, had been right in that.

His hand holding the candlesnuffer shook slightly and he laid it down, the candle still burning. Jules. The brother he had once loved above all others and trusted above all others, until the night he had discovered just how corrupt his family had become. Oh yes, he had tried to eradicate the memory with his own shocking behavior. Jules had called him a fool. Perhaps he had been a young fool, but at eighteen there had seemed to be no other course open to him. Now it was too late.

His course had been chosen. His mind was made up. The pain he felt when he looked at Juliana was nothing to the pain he'd endured for years. His grandparents would have to be disappointed. He found he couldn't offer for any chit just to please them. Juliana's softness, her sweet response in the garden pulled at the pain in him and suddenly he wasn't so sure which pain was the greater.

He was a fool to think that she could overlook the dark secrets of his past, the whispers that would follow her about his reputation. Yet, strangely, he couldn't bring himself to say the words that would push her away from him forever.

The candle had sputtered out on its own and the room was now dark. Dominic walked through the library doors and confidently shut them behind him.

Fool he might have been. But he was not fool enough to ride alone with Juliana. Tomorrow a groom would accompany them.

Chapter 10

Juliana woke early. The sweet anticipation of her ride with Dominic led her to avoid the breakfast room and wander out into the kitchen garden. The day was full of promise: sunshine already overrode the remaining clouds of dawn. She strolled through the neat rows of vegetables and marveled at the difference she felt within her. Dominic had kissed her again! And, although he had seemed a bit distracted afterwards, he *had* asked her to ride with him. She was not feeling alone now.

"Juliana," a voice cried out from behind her.

She looked back to the house. George and Charlotte walked purposefully toward her.

"You're up awfully early m'dear." George smiled happily at her. "Like to join us?"

"Yes do," Charlotte offered impulsively. "We're going to visit the succession houses this morning. Then later we're going to tour the home farm and have a picnic lunch."

"I'm sorry but I have other plans." Juliana shook her head, she knew they would rather be alone anyway.

She watched them walk away. Charlotte pointed at a huge rhubarb plant and gently placed her hand on George's arm. He laughed at her enthusiasm, then took her hand in his and they walked off companionably.

Juliana smiled to herself, satisfied that all was right with her world. No one would be alone—Rodney and Aunt Sophia, herself and Dominic, and now it looked very much like George and Charlotte.

Sophia and her future mother-in-law were seated next to one another on the periwinkle blue damask sofa in the library of the Towers. Sophia felt very much like the early Christians must have before they faced the lions. The duchess had such a sweet smile but what a tongue! Sophia had actually felt herself blush with embarrassment three times already, but this time Rodney's mother had gone too far!

"Your Grace," Sophia said softly, forcing herself to remain calm. "The question of my producing an heir for Rodney has never been discussed between us."

"It should have been!" the duchess declared. "All I want to know is ... is it possible?"

"Yes." Sophia snapped, completely flustered. "But..."

The duchess held up her hand. "I have said my final word on the subject. Only wanted to know if I'm at last going to have another grandchild. Been quite awhile you know. Dominic is twenty-nine."

"I should think, Your Grace, that you might be setting your sights on becoming a great-grandmother," Sophia said brightly, happy to turn the subject elsewhere.

"I have been giving it a great deal of my attention. I thought Charlotte would do. Family connection and all, even if her mother is a horror. Was wrong though," said the Duchess with a decisive sniff. "Charlotte obviously isn't interested."

"And Dominic?" Sophia asked eagerly, curious to know if the duchess was as shrewd as she appeared.

Sophia felt absurdly young when the duchess eyed her sternly. "You know as well as I do where his interests lie. They were both glowing when they came back from the gardens. Haven't seen Dominic look like that since before..."

Shaking her head, the duchess suddenly looked every one of her seventy years. "I have been quite concerned about Dominic's matrimonial prospects. He could have had any chit in the *ton* with a snap of his fingers when he was younger. Now ... well ... I still have some influence. But he's never shown the slightest inclination. Until this."

The duchess's fingers shook ever so slightly when she lifted the gold-edged teacup to her lips and sipped deeply. Sighing, she continued, "Juliana would be a suitable match. Fine family.

Beautiful young widow, but it won't do. Charles saw to that. Soiled goods, that is what Charles would have called her. Disgusting phrase, I know, but one on which Dominic was brought up. His father and mother ruined him for her. God forgive them."

Juliana pressed herself against the roughness of the stone wall outside the open French doors to the library, her hands clenched to her stomach. She had not meant to eavesdrop, but when she had walked onto the stone terrace, her aunt's voice linking her name to Dominic's had drawn her. She had never dreamed that what she learned would drive away the brightness of the sun and the beauty of the day. She was filled with a cold emptiness. Just this morning she had thought this emptiness gone forever, remembering all that had happened in the garden. It had been a miracle—believing Dominic felt something real for her. And now this.

How could his grandmother say this? Soiled goods? Ruined? He was ruined—for Juliana or for any woman? He couldn't be ruined. They wanted him in the House of Lords. Juliana had seen all the lures cast him in London. So it wasn't Dominic's fault. Then it must be hers. Confused beyond bearing, she pushed herself away from the wall and stumbled across the terrace, eager to put distance between herself and the hateful words she had overheard.

Bucephalus pawed restlessly upon the cobbled stable yard when Juliana arrived. Dominic, holding the reins of an ebony mare with a white blaze across her forehead, was turned away speaking to the groom and did not even see her.

Miserable and near tears, the duchess's words ringing in her ears, something broke inside her. Snatching Bucephalus's reins from the startled stable boy, Juliana threw herself onto the nervous horse and thundered out of the yard before anyone could stop her. She heard shouts but didn't let up in the slightest, instead she urged the magnificent stallion out into the Kent countryside.

Bucephalus broke into a crisp, steady gallop that loosened her curls to stream out behind her.

A low wall loomed suddenly in her path, but Juliana felt

no fear as the horse obeyed her touch and sailed easily over it. Once she glanced back over her shoulder, but no pursuer was in sight. Later she would face Dominic and apologize for taking his horse. Now she just needed to be alone.

The wind whipped at her face. She left the path, not wanting to meet anyone. Mile after mile she rode through lush fields and glades rippling with high grass and summer flowers. Finally she spied a small stream. Slowing Bucephalus to a walk, she crossed a narrow covered wooden bridge. On the other side, cut in a wide green hollow, was a flat pasture through which the stream wove, deep and slow between clay banks. Rooks cawed by their nests in the big trees along the water. The branches rustled overhead casting downward a light-leaved net of shadows. No other creature was in sight.

The sweetness of the air, the newly washed smell of everything, the thrushes going wild in the hawthorns, conspired to draw her to this peaceful haven. Sliding off Bucephalus's back, she patted his muzzle.

"What a wonderful animal you are," she muttered before wrapping the reins around a narrow sapling. She left him grazing in the soft grass and went to sit on the bank. Her hat hung heavily on her neck, so she flung it aside and laid down in the lilies of the valley growing wild under the trees. For only a moment she would enjoy the beauty around her and let it hold at bay all the dark thoughts crowding the edges of her consciousness. She welcomed the warmth of the summer's day, although it made her feel drowsy. She had barely closed her eyes all night, so now sleep came and with it welcome forgetfulness.

She hadn't heard him approach. The first she was aware of his presence was his hoarse voice calling her name and his hands roaming freely over her person.

Her eyes snapped open and she sat bolt upright in shocked recoil. "How dare you while I sleep!"

Finding herself once more laying in the flowers, but now imprisoned in Dominic's arms, she felt his hard chest shudder and then, incredibly, heard laughter.

"Why are you laughing?" she demanded, confused, her

sleep-numbed thoughts trying to focus properly.

"Asleep!" he sputtered. "I thought the damn horse had thrown you! I was feeling for broken bones. I've been searching for you for hours."

She suddenly focused on Dominic. A lock of his hair had fallen forward, half hiding his face, and the sun, splashing light through the moving leaves, sent sparks of color through the gold. He couldn't be ruined. He was the wonderful man who had brought her back to life. He had made her face herself and realize she could begin again. Everything, anything could be overcome in the wonder of his arms. Biting her lower lip, she tried to stop giggling in response to the look in his sparkling eyes, but failed and was forced to bury her face in his shoulder as she, too, shook with laughter. They lay together, their mutual laughter and his soothing touch slowly melting the emptiness inside her.

Dominic recovered first and turned his head to look solemnly into her face. They were so close his breath fanned her cheek. His shirt lay open at the throat, a pulse beating strongly in the hollow of his throat. There was a faint moist sheen on his skin. She watched his cornflower eyes slowly darken to navy.

"You should never have ridden Bucephalus, Juliana. He might easily have thrown you. When I saw you laying here I…" he broke off, such a look of concern hardening his features, Juliana's breath caught in her throat.

"Would it really matter so much to you, Dominic?" she asked quietly. So much depended on his answer. Would it be the glib reply of the rake? Or would it be the answer of the man she had come to love?

He surprised her with a heart-stopping smile. "Matter to me! You have haunted my thoughts night and day for years. Of course, it matters to me!"

Breathing the flower-scented air deeply into her lungs, she laughed joyously. His grandmother was wrong … everything was all right. Nothing was ruined.

He must be as bemused with love as I am, she thought, for I couldn't possibly have haunted his thoughts for years. We only met weeks ago.

Yet, she too felt as if he had always been there in her heart. And she would obey Mrs. Forbes. She would do what her heart demanded. Turning in his arms, she placed her lips at the spot on his neck where a pulse beat rapidly. He became very still while she worked her way up to nibble on his earlobe before moving across his cheek to his lips. She touched them lightly and then more deeply realizing that this, not the sweet air, was her breath of life.

With gentle hands he moved her so he could gaze down into her dreamy face, his beautiful hand drifting slowly over her body. Bending, he parted her lips in a deep kiss; she was filled with such longing she couldn't help arching her back to press closer to him. His mouth covered hers again and again, his deft fingers playing in the curls at her neck.

"You're so soft, love," he whispered wonderingly.

Juliana had never known what uncontrolled desire was, but she felt it now, like liquid heat flowing through her veins. Lifting her body into his, she sought his mouth, then moaned gently when she found it. He did love her. She could feel it each time he kissed her.

His breath was sweet as he dragged his mouth over hers slowly. "Oh, love ... I want you."

He bent to bury his face in her neck and she gathered him even closer.

"I want you too ... I love you. Please ... please let us be married soon..." Her breath came in a tattered gasp. "I don't think I can wait much longer."

His arms tightened painfully about her, and he became so utterly still it was as if he had even ceased breathing. Then he moved, supporting himself on hands placed on either side of her face and raised himself to look into her eyes. Some strong emotion she didn't recognize blurred his features.

"Juliana ... Juliana, I want you." His voice was gentle, but it held that same note she had first heard in Mrs. Forbes's parlor and had never been able to understand. "More than I have ever wanted anyone. But there can be no marriage between us."

His words struck her like a blow, but she did not flinch, only stared at him for a long moment before finally understanding all that this meant to her.

Mrs. Forbes, you were wrong!

What had she done? She was sunk beneath reproach.

"Will you please move so that I may get up?" she asked in a cold voice, which matched the chill once again causing her insides to shudder. She would never let him know how he had destroyed her with his callous words.

She was released swiftly, her body feeling weightless without the warmth of him pressing against her. Slowly sitting up, she pulled her chemise back into place. Soon the shame and disgust with herself would settle firmly in her soul, but for now she felt strangely detached, even when he brushed her hands aside to finish the fastenings her fingers were unable to accomplish.

Ignoring the hand he reached out, she stood alone. Without looking at him, she walked to where the mare grazed.

"Juliana!"

The pain in his voice made her stop, but it was a moment before she could force herself to turn and face him.

Even through her own misery she responded to the unhappiness and loneliness she recognized on his face. How did he do it? Time and again he could raise her to the heights and then drop her to despair. With but a look he would beg forgiveness—and she would be within an instant of granting it. The gossips were right. He was a debauched rake unworthy of her. This time he had gone too far. He had stolen a part of her honor and she would never forgive him. She twisted the reins in her hand refusing to ask for his assistance.

"You don't understand, Juliana." He shook his head, his eyes never leaving hers. "If only I could tell you, you would understand why I do this."

She felt her mouth twist unhappily as a tear threatened. She backed up into the velvet warmth of the horse. When she was safely in the saddle she answered. "I do understand ... I do. It is because I am a widow. The Marquis of Aubrey could never marry soiled goods."

She thundered off and his protests were lost in the echoing hoofbeats.

Chapter 11

Juliana fled to her bedchamber, locked the door, and, exhausted, fell to her knees beside her bed. She wept until there were no more tears left, only a bitter burning ache that threatened to remain with her forever. Because she loved Dominic, she had thrown away every rule she had lived by ... her honor, when she broke her promise to Sir Timothy ... and her unquestioned conviction that the intimacy of her love would be given only to the man she would wed. She would have allowed him to love her there in the bank of flowers because her feelings for him were as infinite as the air she breathed. But he only wanted her; fool that she was, she had thought it was love. She had followed her heart ... declared her own love openly and freely and he...

She forced herself to the wash stand where she poured cool water from the earthen pitcher over her wrists. Then she splashed water on her hot face and throat, hoping to still the sickness waiting to overcome her. It was little help. She flung herself onto the twisted covers and buried her face in the pillow. How easily she had fallen under his spell. He had brought other women to the paradise he had offered her, she realized that, but she had been foolish enough to believe there would be no other after her.

Oh, yes, my lord marquis, your charm is lethal, indeed.

She lay there letting her misery utterly overwhelm her. Her bedchamber door handle rattled slightly but didn't open.

"Juliana, please let me in!" It was Aunt Sophia. "Please dear, just for a moment. I want to talk to you," she called softly.

Scrambling off the bed, Juliana nearly tripped in her eagerness to reach the door. Sophia would help her as she always had in the past. Juliana knew she could count on Sophia. Maybe at last, she would discover what this miserable family secret was all about.

She knew by the look of her aunt's face that her own stumbling and sobbing flight up the staircase had not gone unobserved.

But Sophia offered no false assurances and her face was grave.

She sat on the bed and Juliana ran to her, kneeling at her feet.

"Please tell me what is wrong with Dominic. What did Lady Grenville mean in the coach? And the Duchess?" Juliana grasped her aunt's hands. "I heard you both talking in the library. Please help me to understand."

"Oh, darling, I'm so sorry." Sophia shook her head, her lips tight, the skin on her cheeks drawn tautly over the bones. "Come sit beside me," she said gently, pulling Juliana up and urging her onto the bed. "I can only tell you it has something to do with Dominic's mother. Rodney confided in me weeks ago about Dominic and his parents. It is a painful memory for all of them to bear. I think … Rodney was upset with himself for telling me. But I promised the story would go no farther."

"I assumed his parents were dead. What is it?" Blinking back fresh tears, Juliana leaned closer to her aunt. "I love Dominic. I would never do or say anything to harm him. You know that."

Sophia stood and paced to the window, staring out for several moments before striding quickly back to where Juliana waited. Nodding, she took a deep breath. "I know that I can place this in your keeping, my dear. I will tell you what I know."

"No, Sophia, I shall tell her."

Neither of them had noticed they had left the door slightly ajar and now the Comte de Saville stood there, a stern twist on his thin lips.

"Rod told you only what is known to the family. They do not know the whole truth. I do. For I was there," he said, entering the room and shutting the door behind him. "Now, at last, it is time to put away the past."

Juliana looked at him, her breath suspended in her chest.

She had said those exact words when she had put Will's locket away forever.

"I want to speak with Juliana alone, Sophia," Jules insisted.

Sophia hesitated, narrowing her eyes as she studied Jules's stern face. "I once told Juliana that if ever I met anyone she should be protected from, I would descend upon them like a dragon."

Jules lifted one dark eyebrow and his mouth quirked up at the corner in a smile painfully reminiscent of his younger brother.

Sophia nodded. "I will go to my room to fetch a shawl and then I will take a short walk in the rose garden before I return." Stopping only to drop a kiss upon Juliana's head, she was gone.

Jules placed his hands on the mantel and stood studying his fingertips a moment before looking at her. "You are in love with my brother." His straightforward announcement left no room for missishness.

"Yes, I love Dominic," she replied in a whisper. Although her feelings were numbed, she experienced surprise at the look of relief on Jules's thin face.

"I saw your flight across the terrace and into the stable yard. And I saw you return. You have been hurt by Dominic. But I know he loves you."

"No, he does not!" The pain of saying it aloud was too much to bear and she dropped her head into her hands.

"Juliana, I was there when you went thundering out of the yard on Bucephalus. He was like a madman. It was the fear of a man for the woman he loves. I saw love clearly on his face … just as I did in London at Vauxhall. And last night."

At that she blinked away her tears and looked up. "Yes … I had thought…" Stopping, she bit her lip, taking a deep breath into her chest. She searched Jules's face for answers to the questions whirling through her mind.

He sat onto the bed, close to her but not touching her. "May I tell you a story?" His voice softened. "Not a pretty one. But perhaps … together … we can make it have a happy ending."

This was a Jules she had never guessed existed. Jules possessed his brother's charm. She had seen him weave his spell in London, but she had not witnessed this side of him—gentleness, concern—that was what she saw on his face now. His eyebrow lifted again and she nodded, forcing herself to give him an encouraging small smile.

"It started before Dominic was born. When his father, Charles, met Leticia. My mother."

The note in his voice was identical to Dominic's when he had spoken of their mother. So, at least they shared something, these two who always seemed at odds.

"I was a young child when they were married and we came to live at the Towers." His fingers flexed involuntarily. "I was happy here. And Leticia appeared to be happy. Unfortunately, it was short-lived. Dominic was born within a year of the marriage. And after his birth she moved to the west tower and took me with her. She left Dominic in the nursery with a wet nurse. And she left Charles. Never again did they live as husband and wife. But my mother did not lack for companionship. Her lovers were legion."

Jules rose slowly, going to the window. She could sense how difficult this was for him, heard pain in every word. As his hesitation lengthened, she went to him and touched his arm. "Would you rather not go on?"

"No, it must be told!" he said so firmly she dropped her hand back from him. But he stopped her retreat, gripping her shoulders and pulling her directly in front on him. "I have come back to help Dominic understand what happened the night his father and our mother died. I have tried to tell him before, but he would never listen. Are you brave enough to hear it, Juliana?"

Suddenly she was afraid. She didn't want to know. What she learned would change her life forever.

She had to know.

"Yes, I am brave enough, Comte," she answered at last.

Breathing deeply, he nodded. "Dominic was eighteen and home for a visit from Cambridge. Charles had been drinking heavily. His habit had worsened over the years. And Leticia had also consumed too much wine. A new habit for her. But, her beauty was fading and this was her way of forgetfulness. After dinner Charles insisted on showing Dominic the dueling pistols he would present to him on his next birthday. I had finished at Oxford and was eager to go on an extended tour of Greece, the only place left to me. Being French I could not go to the Continent with Napoleon on the march. Leticia insisted she wanted to be alone with me. I could sense Dominic's hurt that, as always, his mother had no time for him. But I had very few nights left with her, so we went to our suite in the west tower."

Jules stopped and Juliana could see a large vein throbbing in his neck. She started to speak but he shook his head. "Dominic went to his father's bedchamber and watched him load the pistols. They were Mantons: superb workmanship, excellent balance. Perhaps Charles had already gone mad, for he placed the pistols under his arm, grabbed Dominic's arm, and pulled him along to the west tower. Charles beat on our apartment door, but Leticia and I were so engrossed in … a discussion that we hardly noticed until he forced the door."

The hard profile Jules turned to her could have been his brother's; the pain she had seen before in Dominic's eyes. So long a time passed that she thought he would not go on, but finally his words fell into the silence as stones onto a still pond.

"Charles thought he saw something … something he misunderstood. It … it robbed him of all reason. He went mad and shot Leticia. And he would have killed me had Dominic not knocked his hand aside. That is how I lost my eye."

"Your stepfather murdered your mother!" she cried, the horror of it washing over her in waves.

"Yes," he answered, his voice toneless. "But there is more."

The burning behind her eyes was nearly unbearable, but she forced herself to look steadily back into his face. Her heart ached for the young Dominic and for Jules, but she had to know. "Please, you must tell me everything."

Jules nodded slowly, his face set. "So be it. When Dominic finally realized that he could do nothing to save Leticia and had summoned help for me, he ran after his father. Charles had simply walked away from the destruction of all our lives."

Juliana covered Jules's fingers with her own trembling hand. "I'm so sorry."

He didn't seem to have heard her, for he stared blindly into space, his voice dropping to a hoarse whisper. "Dearborne tried to break open Charles's study door but failed. So in desperation, Dominic climbed the creeper onto the second-story balcony and was forcing open the French doors when another shot rang out."

Gasping, she stepped back from him. "His father killed himself!"

"Yes. By the time Dearborne had broken through the door, I had reached the chamber with the help of two footmen."

"But how? You were so gravely wounded!"

He brushed aside her concern, his face a stern mask. "I had to go after Dominic. He had not understood what had happened. God knows I was barely conscious, but I had to be there. And I was … Charles died in Dominic's arms cursing the black widow … our mother. Soiled goods he called her, dirtying everyone and everything around her. And then he cursed me. And Dominic. His dying words were accusations of the foulest…"

"Cursed you! But why?" Juliana demanded. "Why, Jules?"

Now it was Jules who stepped back, turning to face away from her.

"There is something between Dominic and I that must be settled before that particular secret can be placed in your keeping, Juliana." He turned to confront her again and raised his thin hand to wipe the tears from her cheek.

"Try to understand. We all changed after that night. Dominic most of all. He became bitter, selfish … even cruel at times. He has used women, Juliana … much as our mother used her lovers." He smiled gently, shaking his head in wonder. "Until now. Until you. I've watched him with you. Dominic has fallen in love at last. And he cannot deal with it. You see why you need to know this, so you can understand why he is hurting you."

"*Cannot* or *will not* deal with it?" she asked bitterly, drawing herself up with all the pride she could muster. Dominic had been badly scarred, and she cried inwardly for that sad, lonely young boy, but he was a man now and must carve his own destiny. Hadn't she discovered that for herself?

"There is nothing stopping him from loving me except the ghosts from his past. I have put aside my own past to love Dominic. He knows that and has rejected my love."

"You can help me rid Dominic of those ghosts. Help him become whole again. I owe him that. But I can not reach him alone. I need you."

Blinking back her tears, Juliana shook her head, the ache in her chest making it hard to breath. "He knows I love him. I can do nothing more. I, of all people, know that only he can put the past behind him. I don't have the key, Jules. Only you and Dominic can bury your ghosts."

Dominic paced around his room in the east tower. He hated it here. Nothing had been changed in all these years; the furniture was exactly the same as in Jules's room, although Leticia had decorated Dominic's rooms in blue and silver and Jules's in crimson and cream. Everything in this room reminded him of her. He had avoided the Towers because of the memories he could not put behind him. Now he was here and it was worse than he ever anticipated.

Everything had ended here at the Towers. He had been betrayed not only by those who should have loved him, but by himself. He knew that now. Instead of running off to war and earning his gallant reputation—only because he behaved with a recklessness that showed he didn't give a damn what happened to himself—and instead of indulging in every excess that had sunk him to the depths of depravity, he should have remained here, at the Towers, and exorcised his ghosts.

Juliana had meant sanity to him. Yet this afternoon he had betrayed her. He had dragged her down into his private hell. It wasn't fair that he wanted her so much, that he loved her—and couldn't have her. He'd done the unforgiveable, but at least no one would ever know. She could go on with her life. And never again would he be alone with her—to have to face that temptation.

He really was a despicable bastard. Like Jules, his code of honor was lost. Irretrievable.

A knock sounded, and before he could deny admittance, Jules had opened the door and entered.

"*Mon frère*, I am finished with games. We will talk. Now."

His thoughts were so filled with Juliana, he could not muster fresh anger against his brother. "We have nothing to talk about, Jules. Go back to wherever you came from!" Dominic stopped in front of the leaded window. The sunlight streamed in, haloing his blond head, throwing his face into shadow.

"Enough time has passed and enough has happened for you to listen to me now," Jules insisted. "You must hear the truth of that night or you…"

"There is nothing to say! And why would I believe you? I trusted you, my dashing big brother! The only one of them who cared a fig for me, I thought. But you … you were just like them. You lied to me for years! I saw the truth that night, and no explanation you can give will change what I saw … or what followed."

"Dominic, you are not an impressionable young man any longer." Jules approached the window. "I tried to comfort you then. I tried to tell you the truth, but you refused to listen."

"And I still refuse." Dominic turned away, reluctant to get too close to Jules. His hands balled into fists, the old pain and anger returned. "I don't want to go over this again … I want to forget it, and this place, and you."

"If you had been able to forget it, I would not be here. It can never be forgotten. We both know that. But it can be put behind us. If you will but listen to me."

Dominic stared into his brother's face for a long moment and then, quite deliberately, turned away.

"You have to listen! If you don't, there will be no hope for your future, no hope for you and Juliana…"

"Don't you dare to speak her name!" Dominic turned back to his brother, anger finally rasping his voice. "You, of all people, know that she is far above both of us."

Jules reached forward, and for the first time since that night, touched Dominic. "Let me help you to understand, then you will see there is nothing to stand between you and Juliana."

Dominic flinched. "You are the one who doesn't understand. After that night ... too much has happened for a woman like Juliana to want me."

"Tell that to her." Jules laughed in derision. "Can't you see that it is only your stubborn pride that keeps you from happiness? Juliana could be the saving of you."

"But at what price to herself?" Suddenly all his anger drained away and he was filled with emptiness. "Juliana has had the love of the most decent man I have ever known. How could I insult her by offering her myself?"

Dominic crossed to the doorway and ushered Jules out. "Leave me to find what little peace I can. We have said all there is to say to one another long ago."

Jules turned to him for the last time, his face hard, his mouth curled in a sneer. "You are being a fool! When you finally come to your senses, you know where I am."

Dominic stood, staring blindly at the door he had just closed against his brother. He could never go to Jules's room in the west tower ... the scene of all his nightmares.

Chapter 12

Rodney and Sophia's happiness was contagious. For their sakes, Juliana tried to enter into the spirit of the house party. Her efforts were noted by all; unfortunately even Lady Grenville was heard to remark that Juliana didn't "seem quite herself."

George and Charlotte did their part by insisting she tour the succession houses with them for one whole day. The duke kept her occupied at the whist table the next afternoon when two of his cronies came to visit.

But she had to be with Dominic at mealtime. Then her forced gaiety was even noted by Lord Grenville, who roused himself to look wonderingly at her.

Sophia felt strongly that Juliana shouldn't be making such an effort when she was obviously so miserable. They were alone in the upstairs sitting room, where Juliana felt certain Dominic would never invade her privacy. Sophia made several desultory remarks as Juliana stared vacantly out into the gardens.

"I don't suppose you've noticed, my dear, but Dominic isn't happy either," Sophia finally managed. "Don't you think you might speak to him? It is a bit disconcerting to the rest of us when you leave a room the moment he enters."

"Yes," Juliana sighed. "Perhaps I should leave the Towers. I'm spoiling everything for you."

"Oh, no, you can't!" Sophia replied promptly. "You can't run away, dear. It would do no good. Rodney says he has never seen Dominic look so haggard." Sophia could see from the hurt in Juliana's eyes that she was as aware of Dominic as she had ever been.

Juliana cast her a speaking glance.

"It's his own fault, Aunt Sophia. I've tried everything..."

she broke into tears.

"Now, now dear," Sophia soothed, "I'll think of something." She brightened. Before she could enlarge on this, there was a knock on the door.

Juliana started and colored up. "No. I cannot see him!" she blurted out.

Sophia rose to admit Dearborne, who formally presented a white note on a silver salver to Juliana.

Sophia noticed that Juliana's hand shook when she read it. "There will be no reply, Dearborne," her niece said with quiet dignity.

He retreated with no expression, the perfect butler.

"What is it, darling?" Sophia watched anxiously as Juliana rose and crossed to the window.

"It was a note from Dominic. He wants me to meet him so we can talk." She flung back her head, laughing, and Sophia crossed the floor quickly to touch her shoulder. There had been a thin edge of hysteria in her mirth.

"Are you going?"

"No!" A hand that shook, crumpled the note and tossed it aside. "I can't!"

Even when George was called back to Wentworth Park because of some problem with field drainage, Juliana didn't get upset— all her months of planning for just the short time he had spent in the *ton* didn't seem important now.

She roused herself to go to the front steps to say good-bye to George. Charlotte was before her, whispering urgently to him as his horse pawed the driveway. Diplomatically Juliana left her brother and Charlotte alone for their good-byes. Only after Charlotte had slipped quietly back into the Towers did she step forward to take her brother's hand.

"I'm sorry to be leaving so soon, Ju. Already made my apology to their graces. Be back in the city before you know it," George forced optimism into his voice. "Don't know what the matter is, Ju, but you'll see. You'll come about."

Knowing he was eager to see her smile, she embraced him warmly. "Have a safe journey, darling. And don't be concerned with me. Aunt Sophia and I shall see you in London within a fortnight."

He was climbing upon his horse when Dominic appeared astride Bucephalus. Juliana quickly moved back into the shadow of the doorway where he could not see her. He leapt down from the saddle and placed a hand on George's shoulder. She noticed that the exertion of his ride had caused his hair to curl and added fresh color to his face. He looked so young and strong, no hint of the dark secrets that tormented him. Why couldn't he always be this way?

The men shook hands and then Dominic stood watching until George's horse became lost behind the beech trees.

When he turned toward the door, he saw her leaning out to catch the last disappearing glimpse of George. They stared at each other wordlessly.

When she could bear it no longer, she lowered her gaze and returned into the safety of the Towers.

That evening a second note arrived.

Three times more Dearborne knocked on her door with a note and three times she told him there would be no reply. She was honest enough with herself to admit why she wouldn't meet Dominic. She wasn't sure that she wouldn't just cast herself into his arms, willing to accept whatever he offered.

The final evening had been declared a family party. Juliana knew Sophia expected the formal announcement of all her wedding plans. She and Rodney had spent interminable afternoons with the duchess hashing out the details.

Sophia confided that Rodney's patience was wearing as thin as his waistline with the Duchess's insistence on near perfection. But it was done and only her aunt's twinkling hints about two dozen turtledoves compelled Juliana to attend the dinner.

A flustered Mary arrived at her bedchamber. "Miss, I'm ever so sorry. Dearborne says they need me in the kitchen." The little maid tossed her head. "Told old high and mighty that me job was to help you, but he was right nasty, he was. Will you be all right, miss? Here, I'll lay this turquoise gown out and be back as quick as can be."

Juliana missed Mary's continual chatter and sat at her mirror playing idly with her curls. She could easily dress herself, but had fallen into the habit of allowing Mary to do everything. When she heard the door open, expecting Mary, she glanced up smiling, but then blanched, for Dominic stood in the doorway. She couldn't move even as he closed the door partway and came toward her.

"I know you're expecting Mary, but she has been unavoidably detained in the kitchens."

Juliana rose, drawing her muslin wrapper closer. "What do you want, Dominic?"

"We need to talk." Strong emotion darkened his eyes and roughened his voice.

"If I'd wanted to talk to you, I would have answered your notes. We said all that needed to be said days ago in the meadow."

Dominic folded his arms across his chest. "No, there is more, much more that you need to know. And I'm not leaving until you hear it."

"I already know about your father. And your mother. Everything." Seeing the look of blankness in his eyes, Juliana felt a wave of remorse rush over her. She didn't want to hurt him! She loved him!

She moved to the window and stood, nervously fingering the fabric. "I understand your father's feeling about ... about widows being soiled goods, but..."

"Never say that again!" he interrupted fiercely, taking her by the arms and turning her to face him. "I would kill anyone for saying that about you. Don't you know why I came here? I've hurt you ... I can't bear that."

Putting his hands lightly against her cheeks, he tilted her face up and their eyes locked. "You are the most wonderful, the most precious ... you are perfect."

Putting her away from him, he shook his head. "You don't

understand what I am saving you from."

"I don't wish to hear any more about my not understanding!" Juliana burst out, drawing herself up proudly. "It is you, who do not understand! I made a promise to Sir Timothy that I would never forget Will. That I would put no one else in his place." She gave a short laugh. "I kept that promise quite well for five long years, but within hours of meeting you, I could not keep you out of my thoughts." Juliana's eyes searched his face. "You see, I love you more than my honor. I have overcome my past ... the teachings of a lifetime ... to love you."

Standing quite still, Dominic's eyes, dark and fathomless, rested upon her. "Do you know what an unsuitable marriage is, Juliana?" His voice hardened slightly when he spoke. "It is when one person is trapped in the net of another's grand passion. It happened to my mother and father. It destroyed them both ... and Jules ... and me."

"I am not your mother!" Juliana, tears finally spilling over her face, said in the only voice left to her, a thin, reedy sound.

"I know," he said quietly, color coming to mark his cheekbones. "But I am her son. I am the soiled goods. Let me tell you what I am saving you from."

She stepped back, sudden fear making her tremble.

"Hear what I am. I would have seduced you at Vauxhall, Juliana. I have done it before in that very same temple. I have engaged in excesses you could not even imagine. I ran away to the Peninsula ... away from my tainted heritage ... only to blacken my name..."

Shaking her head, her eyes clung to his face, which resembled a beautiful polished stone. "Were you hoping to die too, Dominic?"

Amazement that she had understood what no one else had ever guessed shifted in his eyes, but then was gone. "Perhaps at first, but battle suited my needs ... for awhile," forcing as much cruelty in his voice as he could muster. "Then later in Madrid a beguiling contessa taught me much ... things a woman like you would not even understand..." He flinched at the shock on her face, knowing for certain that in revealing his sordid past she would finally turn from him in disgust. But looking into her eyes, shimmering with tears, was his undoing. There had been too much pain already for all of them. He couldn't make himself continue the catalogue of his sins. "I'm not worthy of you. Can never be. I would not degrade you by offering what little I can give, for even that is flawed," he finished softly.

"And that I see, disposes of our future," she said, suddenly furious with him, her chest heaving with indignation. "Do you think you know my feelings better than I do? You are not always right!"

With great deliberation she turned her back on him. "Is that all you have to say, Dominic?"

"Yes," his voice was weary as she had never heard it before. "I wanted you to know that the fault lies with me ... not with you, Juliana. You are all any man could ever hope to find."

She turned to him again. "Yet, you are letting me go."

"You are out of my reach, my darling."

"Only because you make it so..."

"No. Because you are too fine." Unexpectedly he took her hand and led her to sit on the bed. "Perhaps if I had told you this from the beginning you would understand." He paced the length of the chamber considering his words.

"Will and I became friends on the Peninsula. I was with him at Badajoz." Ignoring her gasp, he continued, "I held him in my arms when he called for his Juliana as he lay dying. There in the midst of those bloody battlefields he had spoken often of his young bride. She was so fine, with glorious copper hair, soft and loving, fierce and protective. There, dying in the mud, horror all around him, his vision of you brought him peace. Somehow thoughts of you also brought me peace. And you became my guardian angel. Everything I did in that war, every risk I took, every battle I fought, was for you."

He turned away. "I used to imagine you. Safe in the countryside, the dogs gamboling at your skirts as you strolled through fields of flowers. Or dancing, turning to the strains of a waltz, with hundreds of candles reflected in your eyes."

It brought her happiness to know Will had loved her so.

But that was the past. Now she must fight for her future and her love for Dominic.

"Instead, I was nursing a bitter old man who tried to bind me to the past with promises." She stood and faced him. "As you are trying to do."

He shook his head, rejecting her words.

"Yes," she insisted. "Your vision was just a dream. My life has been far from the perfection you imagined. It's been filled with pain and anger and responsibility. But now, it's filled again with love. And a chance to start over. You must give us that chance, Dominic."

"There is no second chance for me."

Clenching her fists, she rose and stared at him, trying with all the love in her heart to reach out to him. "Why are you doing this? Why are you denying both of us?"

There was a short silence and then, "I am not the right man for you, Juliana."

"You are wrong, you know," she returned quietly. "Nothing you have told me, nothing I have learned, has made me love you less. Dear God, I do not care what you have done. Yesterday belongs to the past. Tomorrow is ours."

He stopped on his way out, turning to face her. That slight hesitation caused hope to flicker in her heart and a new determination to take root in her mind. She would find a way to break through his barriers.

He did not speak, but only lifted her hand and turning her palm up, pressed his lips there before leaving her.

She had been wrong and Jules right. Dominic did love her, and she would not allow him to throw their happiness away. Mrs. Forbes, granddaughter of a gypsy princess, had told her to follow her heart and that she fully intended to do. She had little time left. Tonight she would seek Jules out and discover what she needed to know to reach Dominic. Nothing else mattered.

Chapter 13

Jules had conquered his nightmares. To reaffirm that, he had requested his old rooms during his stay at the Towers. That the duke and duchess had taken great pains to open the rooms again and make them comfortable for him was evident in the faint scent of paint and beeswax.

Dinner had been nearly impossible. Without George, Charlotte was almost silent, except to deflect one or two of her mother's most tiring observations. The duke and duchess tried, with help from Sophia and Rodney, to keep the conversation lively with wedding plans. Even the duchess's grand idea of allowing a dozen pairs of turtledoves to fly overhead in the church during the nuptials, quickly and firmly squelched by the duke, failed to divert. And any chance look at Dominic or Juliana was enough to dampen the evening. Dominic, grim and determined, replied to any observation in a monosyllable; Juliana, eyes brightened with unshed tears, merely smiled and heard nothing. The entire company was relieved when the duchess dismissed them all early to seek their own amusements.

After a brandy by himself in the study, Jules pushed open the door to his sitting room. His valet, holding a thick candle, came out of a doorway at the far end of the corridor.

"I shan't need you. Go to bed," Jules called to him softly.

Alone, Jules passed through the sitting room, entered and closed the door to his chamber behind him.

Inside, waiting for him, was Juliana.

He stopped as if he had walked into an invisible wall. Juliana stood in a gown of softest spring green dimity, her rich auburn hair cascading over her shoulders and down her back, looking for all the world as if she had begun preparing for bed, and then changed her mind.

He came several steps into the room and stood looking at her guardedly.

Her eyes, wide and open in the beauty of her face, rested upon him. "I can't go on like this, Jules. I have come to help you."

She walked toward him, her hands outspread in entreaty. "But first I must know it all, Jules. All of the ghosts that haunt you and Dominic."

"I see," he said. In that moment he paled. He had not expected this and for a moment was set adrift. Finally he moved to stare down into the fire, his fingers resting lightly against the mantelpiece. "Why have you decided to help me?"

"Because I love Dominic. And it seems … what I feel for him … he also feels for me. But there is something keeping us apart. Something besides his rakehell past which makes him feel unworthy of me."

Jules turned from the fire and sank into the depths of the deep crewel wing chair beside it. He knew Juliana could not clearly see his face in the dimly lit chamber.

"I'm sorry, Juliana. But I was wrong and you were right. We cannot help Dominic. Only he has the key."

Juliana's face muscles trembled, but she stilled them. "I cannot let him throw away this gift we have been given."

"There is only one person who can finally put a stop to the legacy of pain our parents left us. And it is not me. Or you," Jules said, not unkindly, after a short silence.

At that Juliana turned to the fire and sank down before it as if seeking its small warmth. "Then you have decided not to entrust me with the truth that will enable me to reach him."

"I find that I, like Dominic, cannot easily lay open that wound to others," he said evenly.

"I see. Then you, like Dominic, choose to continue wallowing in self-pity," Juliana said contemptuously.

He moved swiftly, pulling her up and around to confront him. Then he saw the ceaseless tears pouring unheeded down her lovely face. Jules found that he could not turn away from the appeal in Juliana's wide, tear-filled eyes.

"My mother and Charles were an unsuitable match from the moment they met," Jules began slowly. "They were two people trapped in the net of a grand passion. Leticia's for my late father, and Charles's for my mother. It was a tragedy that grew until it affected everyone and everything around them. For as Charles tried to possess my mother, she became more possessive of my father's memory ... while taking lover after lover. She told Charles she was searching for someone who made her feel as my father had." Jules took a deep breath trying to calm his pulse. Even after all these years it still was not easy.

"After she began to drink, she sometimes imagined me to be my late father, for I greatly resemble him. Charles became so bitter, so disillusioned, that his grand passion turned to hatred. He called her the black widow ... soiled by her marriage to my father. Soiled by her lovers." He hesitated, then the words came swiftly. "Dominic and I were caught in the net with them— pawns in their game of tragedy. Although I tried to keep most of it from Dominic. He was so young then and often away at school, and Leticia spent so little time with him I thought he had been spared the worst. I was wrong. Maybe I made a mistake. It might have been better to acknowledge it, to help him understand."

Jules stopped when he saw the color rise in Juliana's cheeks and her soft mouth begin to tremble.

"Please, I must know how it ended," she whispered.

"That night ... my mother and I fought because I could no longer support her possessiveness. I thought if I went away it would somehow help, make her more receptive to Charles. She ... she became overwrought. She came to my chamber as I was preparing for bed. She had been drinking deeply. She ... she knelt before me, begging me not to leave her ... I think she believed me to be my father." Jules found that he had to turn away from the expression on Juliana's face to be able to continue.

"That is how Charles and Dominic found us ... like lovers." Forcing himself, he once again looked at Juliana. "It wasn't true. Juliana! You must believe me—and make Dominic believe me! Charles went mad and shot Leticia and me. He died believing that Leticia and I were lovers. Cursing us. Cursing Dominic. For in his madness he accused Dominic of being tainted like me. That is why he has become what he is. And this is why he feels unworthy of your love."

Jules's breathing stopped for a heartbeat at the pity in Juliana's eyes.

"There is no guilt for either of you, Jules. Somehow we will make him understand."

Then, for the first time in Jules's life, a woman embraced him in compassion and friendship, and he rested his wet cheek against the fragrance of her hair.

Dominic could wait no longer. His brother had said to come to him for the truth. If there was to be any hope for him and Juliana, it lay in the truth. He knew what that was, but found he couldn't resist taking the chance to change his life. Juliana loved him—any risk was worth taking for that precious gift. He had only to walk to Jules's chamber.

He touched the paneled wooden door to the west wing and found it was not locked. For a moment he heard his father whisper over his shoulder, but he did not look around. Instead, quite softly and steadily he pushed the door open and entered the west wing for the first time since he was eighteen years old.

The quiet and darkness of the corridor was absolute. Dominic Crawford stood in the doorway listening, and allowing his eyes, like a cat's, to enlarge. Slowly, windows grew into his sight, gray against the blackness. Little flares of light in the sky showed him a chest and a large chair placed neatly against the wall. This time he was quite alone. But not then...

His father's grip on his shoulder was sending a hot ache down his arm, but he did not pull away. Instead he quickened his steps to match his father's strides. "Come along, boy. Time we found out how the black widow and her son are spending the evening!" His father's breath reeked of gin and the scent hung about his clothes.

The scent of the corridor was pleasant now. As if the servants had aired it recently and used beeswax on the wainscoting. In the silence his own fitful breathing echoed. It was not how he wanted to sound, but if he could hold back all of the memories, this show of weakness would not matter.

He walked through the dark empty passage and, at last, reached the apartment doors. They were closed, but not locked, he found, and he pushed them open. They had been locked that night...

"Damn her ... damn her to hell!" His father raged, beating against the heavy doors with his fist.

"Father, don't, please!" The young Dominic pleaded and was rewarded with a shove that sent him hurling painfully against the stone wall.

"Leave me be, boy!" His father shouted "I'll be damned if she is ever again going to lock a door against me." With that he began kicking at the latch, gripping the dueling pistols, one in each hand Kicking and kicking until, at last, the lock had surrendered to him. The doors swung open to reveal his wife's sitting room.

Inside it was warm. The flames in the fireplace had sunk to embers giving a rosy glimmer to the room. That night the fire had blazed, lighting the room so that Dominic and his father had immediately seen that the doors to Leticia's bedchamber were open and there were no candles lit within, but the entrance to Jules's room was closed to them.

Tonight Dominic did not look toward his mother's chamber, but instead turned to his brother's room. Then, as now, voices could be heard from behind the wooden doors.

But this time, there was no drunk madman shoving the doors open with such force they shook on their hinges. This time it was Dominic who pushed them wide.

Time ceased to exist, for the door to the past stood open before him.

Two people were in the center of the bedchamber. His brother, shirtless, his trousers half-unbuttoned, his face rigid, an expression upon it Dominic had never seen before. And his mother, her unbound hair falling about her shoulders, kneeling before him, her wet cheek pressed tightly against his thighs. Her hands feverishly stroking the taut muscles of hischest and stomach as she pleaded, "Do not leave me, my darling. I have waited so long for you."

His father screaming, "You slut! You have soiled all of us! Dominic! Jules! All of us! But no more!" The gunfire, the screams, and then, the sudden quiet.

This was the room that held the living well of his torment. All the dark waters of his grief rose and moved to flow over him until in complete surrender, Dominic closed his eyes.

When he opened them two people stood in the center of the bedchamber. His brother, an expression on his face Dominic had never seen before. And Juliana, embracing him, her unbound hair falling about her shoulders, her cheek wet with tears.

He shook his head in denial. He knew what he saw wasn't right. His Juliana would never stoop to this. Out of the quiet a voice spoke.

"You thought you saw something quite different, did you not, *mon frère?*"

Dominic lifted his head to face Jules, and Juliana stepped away from him. By an incredible force of will, she hid her shaking hands in the folds of her gown and stood apart from the brothers, for in this she had no part.

"What are you saying, Jules?" Low and filled with pain, Dominic's voice echoed through the stillness.

"You thought you saw a lover's embrace." Jules looked at him and Dominic paled, and then slowly colored. "You thought you saw our mother ... and me ... in a lover's embrace, didn't you, Dominic?"

Dominic's eyes widened and the bones of his face seemed to sharpen. "She was kneeling in front of you, like a lover. Begging you not to leave her. Father saw it, too. That is why he could bear it no longer."

"I was leaving the Towers to take up residence in Greece. You know that. That is why she was begging me not to leave her," Jules said wearily. "Your father saw only the nightmare his life with her had become. Think back, Dominic. You say I failed in trying to keep the worst from you ... then remember how it was between them!"

As memories crowded into Dominic's mind, clouding the beauty of his eyes, Juliana could almost feel his agony. Jules must have seen it, too.

"The course of misery they set for one another was forged only between them," he continued, his voice softening. "We were only pawns. Until that night. Then we became their victims." Jules straightened and walked forward until he stood directly before his brother. "Once you gave me my life. Now I return yours to your keeping. The taint belongs only to them. Believe me, and close this door forever."

Jules stepped back and turned to Juliana, lifting her trembling fingers, pressing them gently to his lips before walking from the bedchamber.

She had to go to Dominic and offer her comfort. From halfway across the room she could see the jewels on his silk coat sparkle blindingly, showing that he was breathing like a fox bayed down by hounds. He had at some time pushed his hands through his fair hair, for wisps of it dampened his brow. He was as pale as the pristine white of his satin evening shirt. The only color showing in the light spilling onto him was the incredible blue of his eyes. He closed his lids and it was gone.

At the gentle touch of loving fingers on his cheek, he opened his eyes to find his love, his life.

"Juliana?" he asked wonderingly, in the voice she had come to love above all others. "I thought…"

"Dominic, I am here," she murmured softly.

His eyes were clouded a blue she had never seen, but his mouth curved in understanding before he took her hand and held them. "You know what happened here ten years ago."

At her nod he looked away, his eyes moving slowly around the room. "I could believe anything of my mother, and my father. Although I loved them in spite of their faults, as a child will. But Jules … he taught me to ride, you know … and hunt. I, I worshiped him. When I thought Jules was like them, something snapped inside me. Perhaps if I'd been older I could have dealt with the pain. And the guilt that I stood here and let it happen— that I could not, somehow, save … my mother or my father." At last his eyes rested on her face. "At eighteen the only life that seemed open to me was the one I've lived. Because of the actions of that foolish boy, I am considered beyond redemption by the *ton*."

"Is that why the Duke of Monmouth wishes you to take your place in the House of Lords?" she asked gently, sure now that she would allow nothing, and no one, especially ghosts from the past, to stand in her way of happiness.

He did smile then. "Some of the worst reprobates in the *ton* sit in the House of Lords." He tightened his grip on her fingers. "You know of what I speak. The stories are mostly true. My former mistresses litter every social event. The whispers, the gossip, it is not what a man should bring to you."

Pulling her hands from his grasp, she twirled away from him, going to the fireplace to carefully consider the answer that would put his doubts to rest forever.

"The *ton* will soon have something new to gossip about. Something that will make them forget the wicked marquis," she stated firmly, turning to face him.

"Juliana, what…?"

"What am I planning, is that what you are asking, my lord?" Lifting her chin, she folded her arms firmly across her breasts. "They will be gossiping about how I am shamelessly pursuing the Marquis of Aubrey. I shall be relentless."

She paused as he took several steps closer to her. She would not retreat. "And if you should run away to the Continent, I shall follow you. That scandal shall put your exploits to shame."

He stood so close to her now that she had only to reach out her hand to touch him. But she did not.

"You would do this," he said gently.

"For our love I would forsake my pride … my heritage … everything. Won't you?"

Suddenly his eyes cleared, the brilliance startling her. He held back one moment longer before sliding his fingers into her hair; then he bent his head and sought her mouth as a man parched by sun seeks water.

• • •

"Someone do something!" shrieked Lady Grenville as she dashed into the formal salon where the house party had regathered for a late night game of whist. "Dominic and Juliana are in the upstairs hallway and they are kissing as if they will never stop!"

"I am sure they will stop, Mama. In fifty years or so," Charlotte said calmly.

Sophia could watch the emotions chase themselves across Eugenia Grenville's face until her mouth puckered in a pout.

"But that's not fair!" she wailed. "Sophia has Rodney, and now Juliana has Dominic. You don't have anyone!"

"You are wrong, Mama. I shall have George."

Only Rodney's quick action saved Sophia's wineglass from shattering on the floor. Lady Grenville's mouth fell open.

"George?"

"Yes, Mama. I've always wanted George you know. I thought it best to humor you about my Season. I've had it, so now I can go home."

She bowed deeply to the duke and duchess before getting a firm grip on her mother's arm. "I think we should excuse ourselves, Mama. This is now a family party. Oh, Papa, I'm sorry, I almost forgot you were here. Come along, both of you. We must pack."

"But, Charlotte," her mother asked, an anxious note in her voice. "Does George want you?"

"He will, Mama. He will."

As the Grenvilles filed out, the Duchess of Culter turned to Sophia and asked, "Goodness, is the chit serious?"

Sophia smiled, feeling extremely pleased with the whole world. Mrs. Forbes did have the eye! Not even in her brightest dreams had she thought to find such happiness for all of them.

"Sophia, did you hear me?"

"Of course, Charlotte is serious, Your Grace. She never says anything she doesn't mean!"

Epilogue

"I can't believe it! Twins!" Her Grace, the Duchess of Culter, murmured for the fiftieth time as her husband helped her into their traveling coach.

"Yes, dear. A boy and a girl." The duke patted her hand and then turned to take his leave of the couple standing close together on the stone steps. Placing a kiss on Juliana's cheek, he smiled.

"Take care of yourself, don't let Dominic push you to do too much. We wouldn't leave you, but I am sure Rodney needs us desperately. When last I saw him, he was getting thinner as your aunt got plumper."

"Juliana," the duchess stuck her head out of the carriage window, "remember to take a nap every afternoon. We shall return long before your lying-in. My goodness, Sophia gave birth to twins!" she repeated, falling back on the seat.

Dominic's arm tightened around Juliana and she laughed. "Yes, Your Grace, I shall take care of myself. Give Sophia my love and tell her I look forward to seeing all four of them as soon as she can travel."

An hour later, dutifully, Juliana was in bed. She was snuggled in the depths of the great canopied, carved wonder Dominic had ordered from France. And he was there beside her.

He pulled her tightly against his chest so that she could feel the steady beat of his heart under her cheek.

"Are you tired, love?"

Juliana laughed. "I don't think what we've been doing is exactly what the doctor had in mind when he told me to lie down every day."

Dominic's finger gently urged her chin up. His cornflower

blue eyes searched hers; they still had the power to make her breathless. "Should we stop?"

"No! I refuse to be deprived of my pleasure. It will be months yet before I become so ungainly that you will no longer wish to share my bed."

"That will never happen!" Rolling onto his back, he drew her gently on top of him.

"Am I not too heavy for you?" She frowned, for her stomach did protrude and her breasts had become swollen.

"No ... I love it ... I love you," he murmured, brushing her lips gently with his own. Suddenly his magnificent eyes widened. "My God, what was that?"

Juliana laughed again; life was so good. "That was your son kicking."

"Or my daughter ... or, God help us ... both!" His voice was warm with love. "Whatever will we do if we have twins?"

Juliana tangled his thick golden curls in her fingers and bent to kiss him. "Very simple, my darling, we shall all live happily ever after."

THE DUKE'S DECEIT

What if living a lie gives you the life you want to live?

Mary Masterton is a desperate woman. Facing the advances of loathsome suitor she can't imagine marrying, she is short on choices. She convinces a handsome stranger, the victim of a head injury, that they are engaged. Left with no memory of his previous life, the man has no reason to doubt her.

The man's signet ring is the only clue to his true identity as the Duke of Avalon. Determined to reclaim his past, he begs Mary to accompany him on a journey to track down the meaning of the ring. Once more Mary finds herself in a hopeless situation: help the man she has come to love and risk losing him forever, or keep him in the dark and live a blissful lie…

SCANDAL'S CHILD

True love is often scandalous…

As her brother and sister prepare to make their Society debut, Kat Thistlewait vows to sit on the sidelines like a proper young lady. Fate has other plans, though, and when Kat tries to save her mischievous twin she lands herself in a compromising position with battle-scarred and world-weary French nobleman Jules Devereaux.

Knowing that no lady of quality would ever overlook his imperfections, Jules agrees to marry Kat in order to save what little reputation she has left. A marriage of convenience isn't what either desires, but love can grow from the most unlikely of sources.

A SOLDIER'S HEART

Nothing is fair in love or war, especially when they are one and the same.

When the handsome Lord Matthew Blackwood approached her, Serena Fitzwater immediately knew they were meant to be together. Bold and brash, the qualities that made Matthew an excellent soldier made him her soul mate as well. A storybook romance and marriage followed, only to be interrupted by the call for Matthew to return to the frontlines.

When Matthew returns months later, he's no longer the knight in shining armor of Mary's fairy tale dreams. Wounded in action, this man is a stranger. The true battle begins as the lovers must fight to find themselves, and a new happily ever after.

THE CHRISTMAS BALL

The perfect Christmas gift can be found under the mistletoe.

Outshone by a gregarious stepsister and overbearing stepmother, Lady Athena Cummins is used to fading into the shadows. Beloved only by her youngest sister Persephone, Athena has accepted her destiny as a spinster. But Persephone has a different scheme in mind, and conspires to send Athena out for one night of fun at Lord Finchley's masquerade Christmas Ball. The masked beauty catches the Lord's eye but, determined to avoid the wrath of her stepsister, Athena leads Lord Finchley on a wild chase to discover her true identity.

MY LORD'S LADY

For a Lord and a Lady, familiarity breeds contempt—and they are about to get very familiar.

Brought together at the start of the London social season, Lady Georgina and Lord Vane are immediately at odds. The Lord's cool countenance annoys Georgina to no end, while Lord Vane has no desire for his orderly routine to be upended by the passionate Lady Georgina. Forced together while under quarantine, will they overcome their mutual dislike? Are they destined to be at each other's throats…or lips?

Printed in the United States
by Baker & Taylor Publisher Services

Printed in the United States
by Baker & Taylor Publisher Services